DIARY OF A SEDUCER

SOREN KIERKEGAARD

Diary
of a Seducer

Translated from the Danish, with an introduction, by
GERD GILLHOFF

FREDERICK UNGAR PUBLISHING CO.
NEW YORK

INTRODUCTION

Although Søren Kierkegaard is known chiefly as a theological and philosophical thinker, he is also the author of a number of works that show him as an aesthete, a poet, a romantic ironist, and a wit. Of these works, the most widely read, at least in the Scandinavian and German-speaking countries, is *Diary of a Seducer*. For a better understanding of this short novel, some acquaintance with the complex whole of which it is a part is indispensable. Kierkegaard's first important work, *Either/Or*, was published in 1843 when the author was thirty years old. *Diary of a Seducer* is the last of the "papers" making up Part I.

Kierkegaard's development had three stages: the aesthetic, the ethical, and the religious. When he wrote *Either/Or* in 1842, he had already moved beyond the ethical stage, after having characterized the aesthetic point of view in his magisterial thesis. Before proceeding to define the nature of the religious and to show how the religious sphere may be attained, he first undertook to present a debate between the aesthetic and ethical views of life. The title of the work suggests that the reader is called upon to choose *either* the aesthetic *or* the ethical way of life. Kierkegaard's eventual choice is: neither. The only solution is to make a "leap" into the religious way of life.

During the first two stages of his life, the aesthetic and the ethical, Kierkegaard adopted the method of "indirect communication," employing many different pseudonyms. This method enabled him to detach from his own personality the thoughts he expressed, to give them universal meaning, or to indicate that they could no longer be regarded as his own. In *Either/Or*, Kierkegaard used a particularly elaborate system of disguises. The editor, Victor Eremita, discovers a mass of papers in a secret compartment of an antique desk. Upon examination, they turn out to be two separate manuscripts. The supposed author of one manuscript is a young man with an aesthetic philosophy of life. He is a wealthy man-about-town, unmarried, and idle. His name is never revealed; he is simply identified as A. The author of the second manuscript is identified as William, although Eremita prefers to refer to him as B. B represents the stern demands of the ethical life. He is married, has children, and is a magistrate judge. A's papers are in a chaotic state, whereas B's papers are in perfect order.

The papers of A reveal many facets of the aesthetic outlook on life. They show A to be a person whose life is given up solely to sensual pleasures, to passive enjoyment, which inevitably lead to boredom, disgust, and despair. B's papers consist of a series of letters, which are addressed to A and which express friendly admonition: they defend the social institutions, marriage in particular, and urge A to select a definite career.

Part I of *Either/Or* culminates with *Diary of a Seducer*. At this point, the Chinese puzzle becomes even more intricate. In his introduction to the *Diary*, A asserts that he is not its author, that he came across it by accident, but found it so fascinating that he felt compelled to make a rough copy of it, although he did so in constant dread of being surprised by the diarist. In the preface to Part I, however, Victor Eremita, the editor, expresses the suspicion that A is the author, therefore the seducer. It is as if A finds his own diary so disturbing that he does not dare to admit he is both its author and the protagonist of the story it tells. No doubt Kierkegaard was familiar with similar obfuscating devices in the works of some of the early German Romanticists. In *Either/Or*, he is Eremita, he is A and B, he is Johannes, the diarist, and he is the author of the letters by Cordelia, which are included in the *Diary*.

The creation of *Diary of a Seducer* is intimately connected with Kierkegaard's only romantic attachment, his engagement to Regine Olsen. From 1830-40, Kierkegaard was a theology student in Copenhagen. He was a captivating conversationalist, had a reputation for wit, and because he had published a few newspaper articles, he was regarded as a promising man of letters. During these years, as well as later, Kierkegaard had no financial worries because his father, although he came from a poor family in West Jutland and was fanatically religious, proved to be a highly successful businessman. Thus Kierkegaard was able to dress well, frequent the theater and opera, and buy many expensive books; his father always paid the considerable debts Søren accumulated from time to time.

Søren met Regine, the daughter of a prominent official in the Ministry of Finance, for the first time in the spring of 1837 and was immediately attracted to her. Regine, who was fourteen, felt flattered by the attentions of the ten-year-older man. He fell deeply in love with her and soon began to think of marriage, although he had resolved to lead the life of a celibate. He received an affirmative answer to his proposal on September 10, 1840, but already on the following day, he had a sense of compunction.

All sorts of objections to the marriage awoke in him. He felt that he, with a serious and melancholy nature, was bound to make unhappy a girl who was lighthearted and spirited. He also had fears of being impotent. In his *Journals*, he hints vaguely of physical reasons that would prevent him from consummating the marriage. It is true that he had a weak physique and a feeble constitution (his mother was forty-five, his father fifty-seven when Søren was born). With his strong moral sense, Kierkegaard also believed that he had to be completely truthful with Regine; that would mean telling her that once, while inebriated, he had gone to a brothel where he apparently had had sexual relations, although his memory of the occasion was dim. Whatever the reasons, whether physical or psychological or both, he decided to break the engagement, but he did not have the heart to do so at once. The engagement went on for nearly a year; he was often at the Olsen house, and he wrote Regine love letters. Yet all the time, he knew he would not marry her.

It was not until the late summer of 1841 that he sent back the ring she had given him, accompanied by a note that included these lines: "Above all forget him who writes this; forgive a man who, though he may be capable of something, is not capable of making a girl happy." The final break occurred a few months later. In his *Journals* he describes the scene: "She asked me, 'Are you never going to marry?' I answered, 'Yes, perhaps in ten years' time when I shall have sown my wild oats; then I shall need some young blood to rejuvenate me.' That was a necessary cruelty. Then she said, 'Forgive me for the pain I have caused you.' I replied, 'It is for me to ask forgiveness.' She said, 'Promise to think of me.' I did so. 'Kiss me,' she said. I did so, but without passion. Merciful God!"

In 1843 Regine Olsen became engaged to Fritz Schlegel, a civil servant, whom she married in 1847 and who eventually was appointed governor of the Danish West Indies. Søren and Regine never ceased to think fondly of each other, and they exchanged friendly greetings whenever they met in the street or in church. They saw each other for the last time on March 17, 1855, shortly before she accompanied her husband to the West Indies and about eight months before Kierkegaard's death. Her own death occurred almost fifty years later, in 1904.

The papers in Part I of *Either/Or* are to a large extent expressions of the "necessary cruelty" that Kierkegaard felt obliged to apply in order to make Regine forget him or at least turn away from him. In one paper, Kierkegaard discusses three stages of sensuality, illustrated with examples taken from Mozart's operas. In another, he presents psychological analyses of three victims of faithless lovers in stage works, Marie Beaumarchais in Goethe's *Clavigo*, Gretchen in Goethe's *Faust*, and Donna Elvira in Mozart's *Don Giovanni*. But it was the *Diary of a Seducer*, more than any other composition, that was intended to repel Regine and cure her of her love for him. In this story he presents elements of his own engagement in poetical disguise: Johannes is Søren and Cordelia is Regine.

Johannes, the diarist, is a reflective seducer. Although an eroticist, he is quite different from the Don Juan of Mozart's opera, for whom life is a succession of amorous conquests. What fascinates Johannes is the method of seduction, the "how," rather than the number of seductions, the "how many." And he is not eager to make a conquest until he has encountered a woman who will respond to the play of his great intellectual powers. There is nothing modest about Johannes; he suffers from intellectual hubris. In one passage he states that no art is needed to seduce a girl, but it requires good fortune to find one worth seducing.

Johannes is a great flaneur, both literally and figuratively. He spends a great deal of time strolling through the streets of Copenhagen and making expeditions into the surrounding countryside. He has a keen eye for feminine beauty, and he is also the possessor of a demoniac glance. Once he has looked into the eyes of a maiden, she becomes his hypnotic victim, she can never forget him; despite the passage of years she will recognize him at once even in a crowd. On one such occasion this demoniac look is so powerful that a foot valet who is accompanying a pretty young girl at a respectful distance totters and falls.

It is not until well on in the *Diary* that Johannes meets Cordelia and accepts the challenge he has been seeking. His goal is to seduce this pure and virtuous girl first by raising her to his own intellectual level and then by managing the affair in such a way that she, rather than he, will appear to be the defier of convention. But there are times when the reader may feel that Johannes is more of a pedagogue than a seducer, more of a prig than a rake. Cordelia is faintly drawn, she remains a pallid creation till the end.

Critics have called *Diary of a Seducer* a sinister work and described Johannes' plan as diabolically clever. Kierkegaard may have been acquainted with *Les Liaisons Dangereuses* by Choderlos de Laclos, which was translated into Danish in 1832, but if there is any connection between the Vicomte de Valmont and Johannes, their relationship cannot be closer than that of distant cousins. Kierkegaard was no seducer. If he enjoyed the erotic-intellectual, it was in imagination only. There are parts in the *Diary* where the reader cannot help feeling that Kierkegaard is "out of his depth," that he is writing about something he never experienced.

A sinister work does not have charm, and the *Diary of a Seducer* includes many charming scenes. These vignettes, which grant us glimpses of everyday life in Copenhagen more than a century and a quarter ago, are a valuable part of the work. In his various encounters with pretty young ladies as well as in his social contacts, Johannes is not always as devastatingly superior as he fancies himself. Despite his intense self-absorption Kierkegaard had the saving grace of a sense of humor, he could poke fun at himself, and if in the *Diary* Johannes occasionally cuts a comical figure, it is surely with the full knowledge of his creator.

GERD GILLHOFF

Randolph-Macon College
Ashland, Virginia

DIARY OF A SEDUCER

Sua passion' predominante
è la giovin principiante.°

Don Giovanni, No. 4, Aria

I cannot hide from myself, I can scarcely control, the anxiety which overcomes me at this moment, when I decide to make for my own satisfaction a fair copy of the rough transcript which I was able to secure for myself at the time only in the greatest haste and with much nervousness. The situation fills me with the same alarm and self-reproach I felt then. Contrary to his custom, he had not locked his secretary, its entire contents were at my disposal. It would be futile, however, for me to try to extenuate my conduct by reminding myself that I did not open a single drawer. One drawer happened to be pulled out. In it I found a quantity of loose papers and on top of them a book in large quarto, tastefully bound. To the side facing me was fixed a vignette of white paper on which he had written in his own hand: *Commentarius perpetuus No. 4.* Again, it would be futile for me to try to make myself believe that if this side of the book had not been turned up, and if the striking title had not tempted me, I should not have fallen into temptation, or at least should have offered it resistance. The title itself was strange, but not so much in itself as because of its surroundings. A hasty glance at the loose papers told me that they contained interpretations of erotic situations, a few remarks about one or another relationship, drafts for letters of a very peculiar character, which later I learned to know in their artistically perfected calculated carelessness.

When now, after having gazed deep into the scheming mind of this depraved person, I recall the situation, when in thought

° His ruling passion/is the fresh young maiden.

I approach that drawer with my eye alert for every subterfuge, I feel very much as a police officer must feel when he enters the room of a forger, opens his hiding places, and finds in a drawer a pile of loose papers with all sorts of specimens: on one there is a bit of tracery, on another a monogram, on a third a line of mirror writing. All this shows him clearly that he is on the right track, and his satisfaction over this is mingled with a certain amount of admiration for these unmistakable proofs of study and industry. My reactions no doubt would have been somewhat different, since I am less accustomed to tracking down criminals and am not armed with—a policeman's badge. I should have felt the full impact of the truth that I was following forbidden ways. At that time I was so taken aback that I was deprived of both thoughts and words, as is usually the case in such situations. One is overawed by an impression until reflection is restored and, manifold and swift in its movements, insinuates itself with the unknown guest and cajoles him. The more reflection is developed, the more swiftly it is able to recover from the shock; like a passport clerk dealing with foreign travelers, it becomes so familiar with the sight of fantastic-looking figures that it is not easily disconcerted. But although my ability to reflect is undeniably very strongly developed, still, in the first moment, I was greatly astonished. I remember vividly that I grew pale, that I nearly collapsed, and how frightened I was that this might happen. Suppose he had come home, had found me in a faint with the drawer in my hands—a bad conscience is indeed able to make life interesting.

The title of the book did not surprise me in itself; I took it to be a collection of excerpts, which seemed quite natural to me, since I knew that he had always pursued his studies with great zeal. It contained something quite different, however. It was neither more nor less than a carefully kept diary. In view of what I had learned about him in the past, I did not feel that his life urgently needed a commentary, but after the insight I now gained I do not deny that the title was chosen with much taste and understanding, with true aesthetic, objective superiority toward himself and toward the situation. This title harmonizes perfectly with the entire content. His life has been an attempt to realize the task of living poetically. With a keenly developed sense for discovering the interesting in life, he has known how to find it, and after finding it, he has constantly reproduced' what he has experienced in a more or less poetical manner. His diary therefore is neither meticulously factual nor plainly fictional, it is not indicative, but subjunctive. Although, naturally, the happenings were recorded after they had taken place—sometimes, no doubt, a long time later—yet they are often presented with such dramatic vividness that they seem to be occurring now and before our very eyes. That he should have done this because he had some other purpose in mind while writing the diary is highly improbable; it is quite evident that for him it has had personal significance only, in the strictest sense. Both the whole as well as the individual parts forbid me to assume that I have before me a poetical work, one that may even have been intended for publication. To be sure, he did not need to harbor any fear for himself in publishing it, for most of the names are so odd that there is not the slightest probability of their being authentic. I do suspect, however, that the first names are the true ones, so that he himself would always be sure to make the correct identifications, while every outsider would be misled by the surnames. This at least is the case with the girl who is the center of interest and whom I knew. Cordelia was her name in real life, but her surname was not Wahl.

But how can it be explained that despite this the diary has acquired such a poetic coloring? The answer to this is not difficult; the explanation lies in his poetic temperament, of which it may be said that it is not rich enough, or, rather, not poor enough, to distinguish poetry and reality from each other. The poetical was the *more* that he himself brought with him. This *more* was the poetical he enjoyed in the poetical situation of reality, and he regained it for himself in the form of poetic reflection. This granted him the second enjoyment, for his whole existence was keyed to enjoyment. In the first case he enjoyed the aesthetical personally, in the second case he enjoyed his personality aesthetically. In the first case the point was that he enjoyed in an egoistic personal way both that which reality had given him and that with which he himself had impregnated reality; in the other case his personality was effaced, and he enjoyed the situation and himself in the situation. In the first case he constantly needed reality as inducement, as impetus; in the second case reality was submerged in the poetical. The fruit of the first stage is thus the mood from which the diary has emerged as the fruit of the second stage, the word "fruit" being used in the latter instance in a somewhat different sense than in the former. The poetical element thus was always present in the ambiguous course his whole life took.

Behind the world in which we live, far in the background, there lies another world. The relation between the two is very much like the one we sometimes observe in the theater when behind the main scene close to the proscenium there is a second scene on the rear stage. Through a curtain of diaphanous gauze, one sees, as it were, a world of gauze, lighter, more ethereal, of a different quality from the real world. Many people who are present physically in the real world are not at home in it, but belong to that other world. But that a man can dwindle away, yes, almost disappear from reality, may have its reason in a state of health or in a sickness. The latter was the case with this man, whom I once knew without really knowing him. He did not belong to reality, and yet he had much to do with it. He constantly traversed it, but even when he gave himself up completely to it, he was already beyond it. But it was not the good that beckoned him away, nor was it precisely the bad; I do not dare say that about him even at this moment. He suffered from an *exacerbatio cerebri,* for which reality did not have sufficient incitement, at most only temporarily. He did not allow reality to crush him, he was not too weak to bear it. On the contrary, he was too strong, but this strength was a sickness. As soon as reality had lost its significance as incitement, he was disarmed; therein lay the evil in his nature. Of this he was aware even in the moment of incitement, and the evil lay in this awareness.

I have known the girl whose story constitutes the principal content of the diary. Whether he has seduced others I do not know, but it would seem so from his papers. He seems also to have been adept in another kind of practice, which fully characterizes him, for he was far too intellectually inclined to be a seducer in the ordinary sense of the word. From the diary one also learns that at times it was something altogether arbitrary that he desired, just a greeting, for example, and for nothing in the world would he accept more, because this was the most beautiful thing the person concerned had to offer. With the aid of his intellectual endowments, he was able to attract a girl, to draw her close to him, without caring actually to possess her. I can imagine that he knew how to bring a girl to the point where he was certain that she would sacrifice everything. When the affair had progressed so far, he broke it off without himself having made the slightest advances, without having uttered a single word about love, without having declared himself in any way or made a promise. And yet it had happened, and the awareness of this was doubly bitter for the unhappy girl, because she was unable to adduce the slightest proof, because she was carried along by the most conflicting moods in a terrible witches' dance, in which she alternately reproached herself, forgave him, and reproached him. And all the time she constantly had to struggle with the doubt that the affair might be nothing but a product of her imagination, since, after all, it had reality only in a figurative sense. She could not confide in anyone, for she really had nothing to confide. When one has dreamed, one can tell one's dream to others, but what she had to tell was no dream, it was reality, and yet, as soon as she wanted to talk about it to another person and relieve her troubled mind, there was nothing to tell. She was keenly aware of this. No one could grasp the situation, she herself could scarcely do so, and yet it rested upon her with an oppressive weight.

Such victims therefore were of a very distinct nature. They were not unfortunate girls who were outcasts or imagined themselves to be outcasts of society, who grieved in a sound, normal manner and now and then, when the heart was full to overflowing, vented their feelings in hate or forgiveness. They had undergone no visible change, they lived in the same circumstances, as respected as always, and yet they were changed, inexplicably, almost, to themselves, incomprehensibly to others. Their lives were not snapped off or broken like those of other girls, they were turned in upon themselves. Lost to others, they sought in vain to find themselves.

Just as one may say of him that his passage through life left no traces (for his feet were so formed that the footprints he made clung to them—thus I best represent to myself his infinite self-reflection), so one may also say that no one ever really became his victim. He lived the life intellectual far too intensely to be a seducer in the ordinary sense of the word. At times, however, he assumed a parastatic body, and then he was sheer sensuality. Even the course of his affair with Cordelia is so complicated that it was possible for him to appear as the one who had been seduced; the unfortunate girl herself may at times have been confused about the true state of affairs. Here, too, his footprints are so indistinct that no proof is possible. For him individuals were nothing but incitement; he cast them off as a tree sheds its leaves—he became young again, the leaves withered.

But what, I wonder, may be the true nature of his inner self? Just as he has led others astray, so, I think, he himself will go astray in the end. The others he has led astray not outwardly, but inwardly, with respect to their inner selves. It is shocking when a man misdirects a wanderer who has lost his way and then leaves him alone in his bewilderment, but what is this in comparison with causing a man to go astray inwardly? After all, the lost wanderer has the consolation that the scene is constantly changing around him, and with each change his hope of finding a way out is renewed. The person who has lost his inward way does not have so great a territory in which to roam; he soon discovers that he is moving in a circle from which there is no escape. This, I think, will also be his fate, but to a far more terrible extent.

I can imagine nothing more agonizing than a scheming mind that has lost the thread of contact with reality and now turns its whole acumen against itself as conscience awakens and it becomes vitally urgent to find a way out of this confusion. It is in vain that the schemer has many exits from his foxhole; at the very moment his frightened soul seems to behold the daylight entering, what looks like an exit turns out to be a new entrance, and like a startled wild animal, pursued by despair, he constantly seeks an exit and constantly finds an entrance, which leads him back to himself. Such a man is not always what one might call a criminal, he is frequently cheated by his own intrigues, and yet a more terrible punishment strikes him down than befalls the criminal, for what is even the pain of remorse in comparison with this conscious insanity? His punishment has a purely aesthetic character; even to say, "His consciousness awakens," would be applying too ethical an expression to him. In his case conscience appears only as a higher consciousness expressing itself in a disquietude which does not even accuse him in a deeper sense, but which keeps him awake, granting him no respite in his barren restlessness. Nor is he mad, for the abundance of finite thoughts is not petrified in the eternity of madness.

Poor Cordelia! She, too, will find it difficult to gain peace. She forgives him from the bottom of her heart, but she finds no rest with doubt awakening: it was she who broke the engagement, it was she who instigated the unhappy denouement, it was her pride which craved the uncommon. Then she repents, but she finds no rest, for then the accusing thoughts acquit her: it was he who used his craftiness to put this plan in her mind. Then she hates, her heart finds relief in imprecations, but she finds no rest. Again she heaps reproaches upon herself, reproaches because she has hated, she who herself is a sinner, reproaches because she will always remain guilty, no matter how crafty he may have been. Hard it is for her that he has deceived her, even harder, one might almost be tempted to say, that he has awakened many-tongued reflection within her, that he has developed her aesthetically to the point where she no longer listens humbly to one voice but can hear many voices at one time. Then memory awakens in her soul, she forgets the fault and the guilt, she remembers the beautiful moments, and she is swayed by an unnatural exaltation. In such moments she not only remembers him, she comprehends him with a clairvoyance which shows how greatly she has developed. She then sees in him neither the criminal nor the noble person, she feels him aesthetically only.

She once wrote me a letter in which she gave her impression of him. "Sometimes he was so intellectual that I felt myself annihilated as a woman; at other times he was so wild and passionate, so full of desire, that I almost trembled before him. Sometimes he treated me as if I were a stranger, sometimes he was all devotion; when I then flung my arms about him, everything might suddenly be changed, and I 'embraced the cloud.' I knew this expression before I knew him, but he has taught me to understand it. When I use it, I always think of him, just as I think all my thoughts only through him. I have always loved music: he was an incomparable instrument, always responsive; he had a range beyond that of any other instrument; he was the epitome of all feelings and moods; no thought was too lofty for him, none too despairing. He could roar like an autumnal storm, he could whisper to the point of inaudibleness. No word uttered by me was without effect, yet it was impossible for me to know whether it would be the one or the other. With an indescribable dread, mysterious, yet blissful, I listened to this music which I myself evoked and yet did not evoke; always there was harmony, always he swept me along with him."

Terrible is this for her, but it will be even more terrible for him; this I can infer from my own reaction, since even I am scarcely able to control the anxiety that seizes me every time I think about the matter. I, too, am carried away into that nebulous realm, that dream world, where constantly one is afraid of one's own shadow. In vain do I often seek to tear myself away from it; I follow along like a menacing shape, like an accuser who remains silent. How strange! He has spread the deepest secrecy over everything, and yet there is an even deeper secret, the secret, namely, that I am in the know and that this has happened in a culpable manner. To forget the whole matter will not be possible. I have sometimes thought of speaking to him about it. But to what avail? He would either deny everything, insisting that the diary was a poetical effort, or he would bind me to silence, something I cannot very well refuse him in view of the manner in which I became aware of his secret. There is nothing indeed which involves so much leading astray and which is so subject to anathema as a secret.

From Cordelia I have received a collection of his letters. Whether it includes all of them, I do not know, but it seems to me that she once intimated she was holding back some of them. I have made a copy of the letters in the collection and will insert them in my manuscript. To be sure, the dates are lacking, but even if they had been available, this would not have helped me much, since the diary becomes increasingly sparing of dates as it progresses and abandons them almost entirely toward the end, as if the story in its progress grew qualitatively significant to such a degree that, although historical

reality, it came nearer to being idea and that for this reason
the time designations became unimportant. What did help me,
however, is that at different places in the diary are found a
few words whose significance I at first did not grasp. By com-
paring them with the letters I came to realize that they provided the motive for these. It will therefore be easy for me
to insert them in the right places by introducing each letter
where the motive for it is suggested in the diary's text. Had I
not followed these leads, I should have been guilty of a misunderstanding, for then it would not have occurred to me, as
now seems probable on the basis of the diary, that at times the
letters followed one another in such rapid succession that she
seems to have received several in one day. If I had followed
my own thoughts regarding these letters, I should have dis-
tributed them more evenly, without suspecting the effect he
achieved by means of the intense energy with which he employed this device, among others, in order to keep Cordelia at
the highest point of passion.

In addition to the complete revelation of his connection with
Cordelia, the diary contains, interspersed here and there,
several short sketches or vignettes. Wherever one of these
was found, the abbreviation N.B. occurred in the margin.
These sketches are in no way concerned with Cordelia's story,
but they have given me a vivid idea of the meaning of an expression he often used, to which I had previously given a different interpretation: "One must never go fishing with one line
only." Had an earlier volume of the diary fallen into my hands,
I should no doubt have encountered a larger number of these
actiones in distans, as he himself describes them in a marginal
notation, for he himself states that Cordelia occupied him to
such an extent that he really did not have time to look about
him.

Shortly after he had deserted Cordelia, he received from her
a few letters which were returned unopened. These were
among the letters Cordelia turned over to me. As she herself

had broken the seals, I feel free to make a copy of them as
well. She has never discussed their content with me; on the
other hand, whenever she mentioned her relationship to Johannes, she would usually recite a little verse (by Goethe, I
believe), which seemed to mean something different according to her mood and the different way this mood induced her
to recite it:

> *Gehe,*
> *Verschmähe*
> *Die Treue,*
> *Die Reue*
> *Kommt nach.**

The letters run as follows:

Johannes!

I do not call you mine, I fully realize that you have never
been that, and I am severely enough punished for having allowed this thought to delight my soul. And yet I call you mine:
my seducer, my deceiver, my enemy, my murderer, the cause
of my unhappiness, the tomb of my joy, the abyss of my
wretchedness. I call you mine and I call myself yours, and
just as these words once flattered your ear which you proudly
inclined toward my adoration, so now they shall ring out like
a curse upon you, a curse in all eternity. Rejoice not at the
thought that it might be my intention to pursue you or to arm
myself with a dagger and thus arouse your derision! Flee
wherever you will, I am still yours; go to the ends of the earth,
I am still yours! Love a hundred others, I am still yours; yes,
even in the hour of death I am yours. The very language I use
against you must prove to you that I am yours. You have pre-
sumed to deceive a human being so that you have become

---

* Go,/then, and scorn/fidelity./Remorse will follow. (*Jery und Bätely,
ein Singspiel*)

everything to me, so that I would stake all my bliss on becoming your slave—I am yours, yours, yours, I am your curse.

Your Cordelia

Johannes!

There was a rich man, he had exceeding many flocks and herds; there was a poor little maiden, she had only a single ewe lamb, which ate from her hand and drank from her cup. You were the rich man, rich in all the splendors of the earth; I was the poor creature who possessed nothing but her love. You took it, you rejoiced in it; then passion beckoned you, and you sacrificed the little I possessed; of your own you were unable to sacrifice anything. There was a rich man, he had exceeding many flocks and herds; there was a poor little maiden, she had only her love.

Your Cordelia

Johannes!

Is there then no hope at all? Will your love never waken again? That you have loved me I know, even though I do not know what it is that assures me of this. I will wait, no matter how heavy time hangs on my hands, I will wait, wait until you grow weary of loving others; then shall your love for me rise up from its grave, then will I love you as always, thank you as always, as before, Johannes, as before!

Johannes, is your heartless coldness toward me your true nature? Were your love, your generous heart duplicity and untruthfulness? Are you then again your true self? Have patience with my love, forgive me for continuing to love you! I know that my love is a burden to you, but the time will not fail to come when you will return to your Cordelia. Your Cordelia! Hear this pleading word! Your Cordelia, your Cordelia!

Although Cordelia did not possess the wide range she admired in her Johannes, still it is apparent that she was not without modulation. Her mood is plainly reflected in each of her letters, even though she lacked a certain clearness in her presentation. This is especially true of the second letter, where one rather senses than actually understands her meaning, but to me this imperfection makes it all the more touching.

April 4th.

Caution, my lovely unknown, caution! To step down from a carriage is not so simple a matter, sometimes it is a decisive step. I could lend you a story by Tieck about a lady who in dismounting from a horse became involved in such an entanglement that this step proved definitive for her whole life. The steps on carriages, too, are for the most part so poorly constructed that one is almost forced to give up all thought of being graceful and to venture a desperate jump into the arms of a coachman or servant. Coachmen and servants are lucky fellows indeed. I do believe I shall seek employment as servant in a house where there are young girls; a servant easily becomes privy to the secrets of such a young miss.

But, for God's sake, don't jump, I implore you! After all, it is dark; I shall not disturb you, I merely stop under this street lamp, where it is impossible for you to see me, and surely one feels embarrassed only insofar as one is seen, but one is always seen only insofar as one sees. Well then, out of regard for the servant who may not be able to offer sufficient resistance to such a leap, out of regard for the silk dress, *item* out of regard for the lace fringes, out of regard for me, let this pretty little foot, whose slenderness I have already admired, let it test itself in the world, dare to trust it, it will surely find a footing. Even though you shudder for a moment, because it seems to be seeking such a support in vain, yes, even though you still shudder after it has done so, quickly have your other foot join it, for who would be so cruel as to leave you suspended in

this position, who so ungracious, so slow in following the revelation of beauty? Or do you still fear some officious person?
Surely not the servant or me, for I have already seen the little
foot, and since I am a natural scientist, I have learned from
Cuvier to draw definite conclusions from its shape. Therefore,
make haste! How this anxiety augments your loveliness! Still,
anxiety in itself is not beautiful, it is so only when one simul-
taneously sees the energy with which it is overcome. Now!
How firmly this little foot is planted. I have noticed that girls
with small feet generally have a firmer stance than the more
prosaic large-footed ones.

Who would have thought that? It is counter to all experience; one does not run nearly so much danger of one's dress
catching when one steps down as when one jumps down. But
then it is always dangerous for young girls to ride in a carriage, in the end they have to stay in it. The lace and frills are
ruined, and that's the end of the matter. There is no one about
who has seen anything. To be sure, a dark figure appears,
wrapped up to the eyes in a cloak; one cannot see from which
direction he comes, as the street lamp shines directly in one's
eyes. He passes you just as you are about to enter the street
door. At the critical moment a side glance pounces upon its
object. You blush, your bosom becomes too full to find release
in a deep breath. There is indignation in your glance, a proud
contempt; there is a prayer, a tear in your eye; both parts are
equally beautiful, I accept both with equal right, for I can
just as well be the one as the other.

But I am being malicious—what is the number of the house?
What do I see? A window display of fancy goods! My unknown beauty, it may be outrageous on my part, but I follow
the bright street. . . . She has forgotten what happened just now.
Ah yes, when one is seventeen, when at that happy age one
goes shopping, when one joins an ineffable joy to every object, large or small, that one picks up, then it is easy to forget.
She has not yet seen me; I stand by myself a good distance

away, at the far end of the counter. A mirror hangs on the opposite wall, she pays no attention to it, but the mirror is aware of her. How faithfully it has caught her image, like a humble slave who shows his utter devotion by his faithfulness, a slave for whom she indeed has significance, but who has no significance for her, who dares to hold her, but not to enfold her. Unhappy mirror, that can hold her image but not herself, unhappy mirror, that cannot conceal her image in its hidden depths from the whole world, that, on the contrary, can only betray it to others, as now to me! What agony, if a human being were thus constituted! And yet, are there not many persons like that, who own a thing only in the moment when they show it to others, who grasp only the surface, never the essence, who lose everything when this is revealed, just as this mirror would lose her image, if she by a single breath were to betray her heart to it? And if a person were unable to hold an image in recollection even when he is present, then he would always desire to be at a distance from beauty, not so close that the physical eye cannot see how beautiful that is which he holds in his embrace and which this eye has lost. To be sure, he can regain it for the outward sight by putting it at a distance from himself, but he may also keep it before the soul's eye when he cannot see the object because it is too close to him, when lips are pressed upon lips. . . .

But how beautiful she is! Poor mirror, it must be torture; it is fortunate that jealousy is unknown to you. Her head is perfectly oval, she bends forward a little, whereby her forehead, which rises pure and proud without any external indication of intellectual faculties, becomes higher. Her dark hair clings tenderly and softly about her brow. Her face is like a fruit, every transition is voluptuously rounded, her skin is transparent, like velvet to the touch; that I can feel with my eyes. Her eyes—well, I have not yet seen them, they are hidden behind lids armed with silken fringes that curve like hooks, dangerous to him who seeks to meet her glance. Her head is the head of a

Madonna, purity and innocence have given it its cast; she bends forward like a Madonna, but she is not lost in contemplation of the One; a variety of expressions are reflected on her face. What she contemplates is the manifold, the manifold over which earthly splendor and glory cast a glow. She removes her glove and discloses to the mirror and to me a right hand, white and shapely like an antique, without adornment, not even with a plain gold ring on her fourth finger—good!

She looks up, and now everything is changed and yet the same: the forehead is a little less high, the face a little less regularly oval, but more alive. She is talking with the salesman, she is gay, cheerful, loquacious. She already has chosen a few things, she picks up another item and holds it in her hands, her eyes are lowered again, she asks what it costs, she places it to one side under her glove; it must surely be a secret, intended for—a sweetheart? No, she is not engaged, but, alas, there are many who are not engaged and yet have a sweetheart, and many who are engaged and yet do not have a sweetheart. . . .

Should I give her up? Should I leave her undisturbed in her happiness? . . . She wants to pay, but she has lost her purse. No doubt she mentions her address, but I do not want to hear it. I do not want to deprive myself of the surprise; I shall surely meet her again in life, I shall recognize her, and she perhaps will recognize me, my side glance is not forgotten so easily. When I shall have been surprised at meeting her in unexpected surroundings, then it will be her turn. If she does not recognize me, if I gather directly from her glance that this is the case, I shall not fail to look at her from the side, and I declare that she will recall the situation. No impatience, no greediness, everything is to be enjoyed in slow draughts. She has been chosen, she will be overtaken.

the 5th.

I like that: alone on Østergade in the evening! Yes, of course I
see the footman who follows. Do not believe that I think so ill
of you as to hold you capable of going out all alone, do not
believe me so inexperienced that in my survey of the situation
I do not at once notice this austere figure. But why the hurry?
One does feel a little anxiety, one is conscious of the beating
of one's heart, which is not attributable to an impatient desire
to reach home, but rather to an impatient apprehension that
courses through one's entire body with sweet unrest; hence the
feet's swift measure. Nevertheless, it is splendid, precious, to
go out alone like this—with the footman following. . . .

One is sixteen, one is well read, that is to say, one is well
read in novels, one has, while happening to pass through one's
brothers' rooms, caught a word or two of a conversation between them and their acquaintances, a word or two about Østergade. Later one has repeatedly flitted through in the hope
of picking up a little additional enlightenment. In vain. It is
only proper, after all, for a grown-up girl to know a little something about the world. If only it were possible to go out, followed, of course, by the servant, without offering an explanation! No, thank you, Father and Mother would be quite taken
aback, and what kind of excuse could one proffer, after all?
When one goes to a party, the opportunity does not arise, for
August was heard to say: about nine or ten o'clock. And when
one goes home, it is too late, and then one is usually saddled
with an escort. Thursday evening, when we return from the

theater, would really offer an excellent opportunity, but on these occasions Mrs. Thomsen and her charming cousins are always crowded into the carriage. If one were riding alone, one could at least lower the window and look about a little.

But the unforeseen often happens. Today Mother said to me, "It doesn't look as if you'll manage to finish what you are sewing for your father's birthday; in order to work completely undisturbed, you may go to Aunt Jette's and stay there till tea time. Jens will then call for you." This was hardly a very pleasant announcement, for it is extremely boring at Aunt Jette's place, but in this way I shall be going home alone with the footman at about nine o'clock. When Jens arrives, he will have to wait until a quarter of ten, and then off we go! If only I encountered my brother or August—but that might not be so desirable, after all, for then I'd probably be escorted home. No, thanks, it is better to be free, to enjoy freedom. . . . But if I managed to catch sight of them without their seeing me?

Well, my little lady, what do you see, and what do you think I see? In the first place, the little cap you are wearing is most becoming and harmonizes completely with the breathlessness of your appearance. It is not a hat, neither is it a bonnet, rather a kind of hood. But you cannot possibly have had it on this morning when you left your home. Could the footman have brought it or could you have borrowed it from Aunt Jette?—Perhaps you are incognito.—The veil should not be lowered completely if one wishes to make observations. Or perhaps it is not a veil at all but only a broad piece of lace? In the dark it is impossible to tell. Whatever it is, it hides the upper part of the face. The chin is quite pretty, a little too pointed; the mouth is small, slightly open; that is because you are walking too rapidly. The teeth are white as snow. That is as it should be. Teeth are of the utmost importance, they are a bodyguard, hiding behind the lips' seductive softness. The cheeks are aglow with health.

If one tilted one's head a little, it would be possible to

penetrate under this veil or lace. Be on your guard, such a glance from below is more dangerous than a direct one. It is as in fencing; and what weapon is so sharp, so penetrating, so flashing in its movements, and hence so deceiving, as the eye? One feints a high quart, as the fencers say, and attacks in second; the swifter the attack can follow the feint, the better. It is an indescribable moment, this moment of the feint. The opponent feels the stroke, as it were, he has been touched, but in an entirely different place from the expected one. . . .

With unflagging perseverance she walks on, without fear and without blame. Be on your guard! Yonder comes a man. Lower your veil, do not let his profane glance defile you! You have no idea, you may find it impossible for a long time to forget the revolting fear with which it touched you—you do not notice, but I do, that he has sized up the situation. The footman has been chosen as the next object. Yes, now you see the consequences of going out alone with the servant. He has fallen down. It is really quite absurd, but what are you going to do now? For you to retrace your steps and help him to get back on his feet is impossible, to be accompanied by a soiled servant is unpleasant, to continue on alone is dangerous. Be on your guard, the monster approaches!

You do not answer me. Just look at me, does my exterior inspire the least fear in you? I make no impression at all upon you. I look as if I were a good-natured person from an entirely different world. There is nothing in my speech to upset you, nothing to remind you of the situation, no movement on my part to cause you the slightest offense. You are still a bit frightened, you have not yet forgotten the attempt of that sinister figure on you. You take a certain liking to me, the embarrassment that prevents me from looking at you directly puts you in the ascendant. It heartens you and makes you feel safe, you might almost be tempted to poke a little fun at me. I wager that at this very moment you would have the courage to take my arm, if it occurred to you. . . .

So you live in Stormgade. You nod coldly and curtly. Have
I deserved this, I who helped you out of the whole unpleasant
situation? You regret your attitude, you turn back, thank me
for my attention, extend your hand—why do you grow pale?
Is not my voice unchanged, my bearing the same, my eye just
as quiet and calm? This handclasp? Can, then, a handclasp
have any meaning? Yes, it can mean much, very much, my
little lady, within a fortnight I shall explain everything to you;
until then this contradiction will remain with you: I am a good-
natured man who like a knight comes to the assistance of a
young girl, and I can at the same time press your hand in a
manner nothing less than good-natured.

April 7th.

"On Monday, then, at one o'clock at the Exhibition." Very well, I shall have the honor of arriving at a quarter of one. A little rendezvous. Last Saturday I finally decided to pay my much-traveled friend, Adolph Bruun, a visit. At about seven o'clock in the evening I therefore went to Vestergade, where I had been told he was staying. He could not be found, however, not even on the fourth floor, which I reached quite out of breath. As I am about to go downstairs, my ear catches the sound of a woman's melodious voice, which says softly, "On Monday, then, at one o'clock at the Exhibition. At that time the others are out, but you know I never dare to see you at home." The invitation was not meant for me, but for a young man, who was out of the door in a trice, so fast that not even my eyes, let alone my feet, could follow him. Why don't they have gas-light on stairways? Then I should perhaps have been able to see whether it would be worth the trouble to be so punctual. On the other hand, had there been light, I should perhaps not have chanced to hear anything. The existent is, after all, the rational; I am and remain an optimist. . . .

Which one is she, I wonder. The Exhibition "swarms with young girls," to use Donna Anna's words. It is exactly a quarter of one. My lovely unknown, may your intended be as punctual as I am! Or perhaps you would prefer that he never come fifteen minutes too early; as you wish, I am at your service in every way . . . "Bewitching enchantress, fairy or sorceress, let your cloud vanish," reveal yourself; no doubt you already are present, but invisible to me; disclose yourself, for otherwise I may not expect a revelation. Could there perhaps be several up here on a similar errand as she? Quite likely. Who knows the ways of man even when he goes to an exhibition?

Suddenly a young girl turns up in the first room, hurrying faster than a bad conscience after a sinner. She forgets to give up her ticket, the red-uniformed man stops her, Good gracious, what a hurry she is in! She must be the one. Why such unseemly impetuosity? It is not yet one o'clock, keep in mind that you are to meet the beloved. Is it entirely unimportant on such occasions how one looks, or does the expression of putting one's best foot forward have relevance here? When a sweet young thing goes to a rendezvous, she attacks the matter like a demented person. She is thoroughly flurried. I, on the other hand, sit here comfortably on my chair and contemplate the charming view of a rural scene . . . She is the devil's own girl, the way she storms through all the rooms. You must endeavor to hide your eagerness a little, remember the words spoken to Mistress Lisbeth: "Is it seemly for a young girl to let it be seen how eager she is to 'get together'?" It goes without saying, of course, that your getting together here is of the innocent kind.

A tryst is usually regarded by lovers as the most beautiful moment of all. I myself still remember as vividly as if it were yesterday the first time I dashed to the appointed place, my heart as full as it was ignorant of the joy awaiting me, the first time I knocked thrice, the first time a window was opened, the first time a wicket was unlatched by the invisible hand of a girl who remained hidden while she opened it, the first time I concealed a girl under my cloak in the light summer night. But much illusion enters into this judgment. The sober third party does not always find that the lovers are most beautiful in this moment. I have witnessed trysts the total impression of which was almost revolting, although the girl was lovely and the man handsome; in such cases the meeting itself was far from being beautiful, although no doubt it seemed so to the lovers. As one becomes more experienced, one gains to a degree, for while one loses the sweet unrest of impatient longing, one wins the poise to make the moment truly beautiful. It distresses me when I see a man on such an occasion become so discomposed that he suffers an attack of delirium tremens from mere love. What does a yokel know about cucumber salad! Instead of possessing sufficient coolness to enjoy her agitation, to allow it to inflame her beauty and render it incandescent, the young man brings about a wretched confusion, and yet he returns home in a joyous state, imagining that he has experienced something wonderful.

But where the devil is the fellow? It is already close to two o'clock. Yes, they are a fine lot, these lovers! What a rascal, to keep a young girl waiting for him! Now I, on the contrary, am a completely reliable person! I guess the time has come to address her, now that she passes me for the fifth time. "Pardon my boldness, lovely lady. Surely you are looking for your family here, you have hurried past me several times, and as my eyes followed you, I noticed that you always stopped in the last room but one, perhaps you do not know that it leads to still another room. You might find there the people you are looking for." She curtsies to me, the gesture becomes her. The opportunity is favorable, I am glad that the fellow has not come; one always fishes best in troubled waters. When a young girl is upset, one can successfully venture a great deal that might otherwise fail. I bow to her as politely and reservedly as possible. I return to my chair, contemplate my landscape, and keep an eye on her. To follow her immediately would be to risk too much, it might make me seem obtrusive, and then she would be on her guard at once. Now she believes that I accosted her out of sympathy, and I am in her good graces.

There is not a soul in the last room, I am quite aware of that, but solitude will have a beneficial effect on her. As long as she sees many people about her, she is upset; when she is alone, she is sure to become calm. It is as I anticipated, she stays in there. In a little while I shall enter the room, *en passant*, as it were; I am entitled to address her again, she owes me a greeting at least.

She has sat down. Poor girl, she looks so melancholy; she has been crying, I believe, or at least there have been tears in her eyes. But be calm, you shall be avenged, I shall avenge you, he shall find out what it means to wait.—How beautiful she is, now that she is no longer buffeted by the winds of conflicting emotions and finds repose in one mood. Her being is melancholy and the harmony of pain. She is really enchanting. There she sits in her traveling clothes, and yet it wasn't she who was going to travel, she put them on in order to go out and look for joy, and now they are an indication of her pain, for she is like one from whom joy departs. She looks as if she were saying farewell to the beloved for always. Let him go!— The situation is favorable, the moment beckons. The thing to do now is to express myself in such a way that it will seem as if I think that she is looking for her family or a group of friends up here, but at the same time so warmly that each word falls in with her feelings; thus I shall manage to insinuate myself into her thoughts.

The devil take him! The man I see approaching undoubtedly is the one she has been waiting for. What bad luck that this oaf should turn up at the very moment when I seemed to have the situation well in hand! Still, one ought to be able to derive some advantage from it. I must find out about their relationship, get myself into the picture. When she sees me, she will have to smile at my believing that she was looking for her family, whereas she was looking for something entirely different. This smile makes me her accomplice, which, after all, is something.—A thousand thanks, my child, this smile is worth much more than you realize, it is the beginning, and the beginning always is hardest. Now we are acquaintances, and our acquaintance is based on a piquant situation; for me that is enough until later. You will hardly stay here more than an hour; in two hours I shall know who you are. For what other purpose do you think the police keep a directory?

Have I become blind? Has the inner eye of my soul lost its power? I have seen her, but it is as if I had seen a heavenly revelation, so completely has her image again vanished from me. In vain do I exert all my soul's power in order to conjure up this image. If I ever get to see her again, then I shall recognize her immediately, even though she were standing among hundreds. Now she has fled away, and my soul's eye vainly seeks to reach her with its longing.

I was strolling along Langelinie in a seemingly casual manner and indifferent to my surroundings, although my watchful eye let nothing pass unnoticed, when suddenly I caught sight of her. It fixed itself unswervingly upon her, it no longer obeyed its master's will; I found it impossible to move it at all and to take in the object I desired to see, I did not see, I simply stared. Like a fencer who rigidly holds a lunging position my eye remained fixed, petrified in the position it had taken. It was impossible for me to lower it, impossible to withdraw it, impossible to see, because I beheld too much. The only thing that has stayed with me is that she wore a green cloak, that is all—what one might call catching the cloud instead of Juno; she slipped from me as Joseph slipped from Potiphar's wife, leaving only her cloak behind. She was accompanied by an elderly lady, who seemed to be her mother. I can describe her from top to toe, and that although I really didn't look at her at all, taking her in only *en passant*. So it goes. The girl made an impression upon me, and her I have forgotten; the other made no impression upon me, and her I can remember.

My soul is still ensnared in the same contradiction. I know that I have seen her, but I also know that I have forgotten what I saw, forgotten it in such a way that the surviving fragment of recollection does not refresh me. With an unrest and a vehemence as if my well-being were at stake, my soul cries for this image, and yet it does not appear. I could tear out my eyes in order to punish them for their forgetfulness. When I have raged impatiently, when calm again prevails within me, then it is as if presentiment and memory wove a picture for me, but one which refuses to assume a definite form, because I cannot get it to remain fixed in a context; it is like a pattern in a fine fabric, the pattern is lighter than the ground; it cannot be seen by itself, it is too light for that.

This is a strange condition to be in, and yet it has its agreeable aspects, because of itself as well as because it assures me that I am still young. This can also be learned from another consideration, the one, namely, that I constantly seek my prey among young girls, not among young women. A woman has less nature and more coquetry, an affair with her is not beautiful, not interesting, it is piquant, and the piquant is always the final stage.—I had not expected that I should be able again to taste the first fruits of being in love. I am immersed in love, I have been given what swimmers call a ducking; no wonder that I am a bit bewildered. So much the better, so much the more I promise myself from this affair.

I hardly recognize myself. My mind seethes like a sea agitated by the storms of passion. If another could see my soul in this state, it would seem to him like a yawl that plunged its prow into the sea and in its awful speed steered its course to the bottom of the abyss. He does not see that high up on the mast a sailor holds watch. Roar, you wild forces, rage, you powers of passion! Even though your crashing waves hurl foam up to the skies, you shall not be able to engulf me. I sit serene like the Cliff King.

I can hardly find a footing, like a water bird I try in vain to alight on my spirit's agitated sea. And yet in such an uproar I find my element; I build upon it as the *Alcedo ispida* builds its nest upon the sea.

Turkey cocks flare up when they see red; so it is with me when I see green, each time I see a green cloak; and since my eyes often deceive me, all my anticipations frequently collapse against what turns out to be the green coat of a stretcher-bearer from Frederik's Hospital.

One must restrict oneself, that is one of the chief requisites for all enjoyment. It does not look as if I shall obtain any information about the girl who fills my soul and mind so completely that my sense of want seeks constant nourishment. I shall now keep very calm, for also this condition, this dark, indefinite, and yet powerful mood, has a sweetness of its own. I have always been very fond of lying in a boat on a moonlit night out on one of our beautiful lakes. I then furl the sails, unship the oars, and take in the rudder, stretch out full length, and gaze up at the vault of heaven. When the waves rock the boat on their bosom, when the clouds drive swiftly before the wind, so that the moon disappears and reappears in quick succession, then I find rest in this unrest; the motion of the waves soothes me, their beating against the sides of the boat is a monotonous cradle song; the swift passage of the clouds, the alternation of light and shadow, all this intoxicates me, so that I dream while waking. In the same way I now lie down, after furling the sails and taking in the rudder, longing and expectation become more and more quiet, more and more blissful; they caress me like a child, above me arches the heaven of hope, her image sails past me like the moon's, indistinct, now dazzling me with its light, now with its shadow. How very enjoyable thus to be rocked on heaving water—how very enjoyable to be moved within oneself!

The days go by, and still I have made no progress. Young girls delight me more than ever, and yet I have no desire to taste pleasure. I seek her everywhere. This often makes me unreasonable, dims my vision, enfeebles my enjoyment.

The beautiful season will soon be here when in the public life on the highways and byways one buys up many a petty claim which one collects with a profit during the winter's social life; for a young girl may forget much, but never a situation. To be sure, social life brings me into contact with the fair sex, but that is not the way to start an affair. In society every girl is armed, the situation is stale and constantly repeated, the girl experiences no sensual excitement. On the street she is as on the open sea, and therefore everything affects her more strongly as well as more mysteriously. I would give a hundred rix-dollars for a smile from a girl in a street situation, not ten rix-dollars for the pressure of a hand at a social gathering; two entirely different kinds of currencies are involved. When the affair is under way, one looks in society for the person concerned. One communicates with her in a clandestine manner that is tantalizing; I know of no more effective incitement. She dares not talk about it and yet her mind dwells on it; she knows not whether one has forgotten it or not; now one deludes her in one way, now in another. This year I do not expect to collect much, the girl preoccupies my mind. In a certain sense my returns will be poor, but on the other hand I have the prospect of winning the grand prize.

Damnable chance! Never have I cursed you because you have appeared, I curse you because you fail to appear at all. Or is this perhaps a new invention on your part, incomprehensible being, barren mother of all, the only survival from that time when necessity gave birth to freedom, when freedom was lured back into the womb?

Damnable chance! You who are my only confidant, the only being whom I deem worthy of being my ally and my enemy, always similar in your dissimilarity, always incomprehensible, always a riddle! You whom I love with all the sympathy of my soul, in whose image I form myself, why do you not show yourself? I do not beg you, I do not humbly implore you to show yourself in this way or that; such worship would be idolatry, displeasing to you. I challenge you to battle, why do you not appear? Or has the balance in the world's structure ceased to vibrate, is your riddle solved, so that you too have flung yourself into the sea of eternity? Terrifying thought, in that case the world has come to a standstill from boredom!

Damnable chance, I await you. I do not strive to conquer you with principles or with what foolish people call character, no, I want to be your poet! I do not want to be a poet for others; reveal yourself, I will be your poet, I consume my own poem, it is my nourishment. Or do you consider me unworthy? Like a bayadere who dances in honor of her god, I have dedicated myself to your service. Lithe, lightly clad, lissome, weaponless, I renounce everything. I own nothing, I wish to own nothing, I love nothing, I have nothing to lose, but for all that I have not become worthier of you, you who long ago must have grown tired of wrenching people from what they love, tired of their craven sighs and craven prayers. Take me by surprise, I am ready; let there be no stakes, let us fight for honor. Show her to me, show me a possibility that seems to be an impossibility, show her to me among the shades of Hades, I shall fetch her up. Let her hate me, despise me, be indifferent to me, love another—I am not afraid. Only let the waters be troubled, let the silence be broken. To starve me thus is unworthy of you, who consider yourself to be stronger than I am.

Spring is here. Everything is in bloom, including the young girls. Cloaks are being laid aside, no doubt my green one too has been hung away. Here you see the consequence of making a girl's acquaintance on the street instead of in society, where one quickly gets to know her name, who her family is, where she lives, whether she is engaged. The last of these is an extremely important piece of information for all sedate and constant suitors, to whom it would never occur to fall in love with an engaged girl. Such a stolid individual would be in dire distress if he were in my place; he would be crushed if his efforts to gain information were crowned with success and yielded the detail that she was engaged. This does not worry me very much, however. An engaged person provides a comic difficulty. I fear neither comic nor tragic difficulties; the only ones I fear are the boring ones. So far I have not learned a single bit of information, despite the fact that I have left nothing untried and have frequently felt the truth of the poet's words:

> *nox et hiems longaeque viae, saevique dolores*
> *mollibus his castris, et labor omnis inest.**

Perhaps she does not live here in the city, perhaps she is from the country, perhaps, perhaps . . . I could become furious over all these possibilities, and the more furious I become, the more possibilities there are. At all times I have money in

---

* Night and winter, long marches and fierce pains,/and all manner of exertion there are in this unwarlike camp. (Ovid, *Ars amandi*)

readiness in order to be able to set out on a journey. I look for her in vain at the theater, concerts, balls, and on promenades. In a way my failure pleases me: a young girl who participates a great deal in such entertainments is usually not worth winning. She very often lacks the naturalness which for me is and always will be *conditio sine qua non*. It is less unheard-of to find a Preciosa among the gypsies than in the public places where young girls are offered for sale—in all innocence, of course, who would say otherwise!

I say, my child, why didn't you remain standing quietly in the entrance way? There is nothing to take exception to if a young girl steps out of the rain into an entrance. I do it, too, when I have no umbrella—yes, sometimes even when I have one, as now, for instance. Besides, I could mention several worthy ladies who have not hesitated to do so. One keeps very quiet, turning one's back to the street, so that the passers-by have no way of telling whether one is standing there or is about to go up into the house. On the other hand, it is incautious to hide behind the door if it happens to be half open, chiefly on account of the consequences, for the more one is hidden, the more unpleasant it is to be surprised. If, however, one has concealed oneself, then one must remain standing very quietly, recommending oneself to the care of one's good genius and all the angels; one should refrain especially from peering out— in order to see whether the rain has stopped. If one wants to make sure, one steps out boldly and looks up at the sky with an earnest expression. But if one sticks out one's head somewhat curiously, diffidently, anxiously, uncertainly, and then quickly draws it back—well, every child understands this movement, it is called playing hide-and-seek. And I, who always participate in the game, I should hold back, I should refrain from answering when I hear the question. . . !

Don't think that I harbor any insulting thoughts about you, you didn't have the slightest ulterior motive in poking your head out, it was the most innocent action in the world. In return, you must not insult me in your thoughts, my good name and reputation cannot bear up under that. Besides, it was you who made the beginning. I advise you never to discuss this incident with anybody; it is you who are in the wrong. What do I intend to do other than what any gentleman would—to offer you my umbrella?

Now where did she go? Capital, she has hidden herself in the porter's doorway.—She is the sweetest little girl, gay and happy. "Perhaps you could give me some information about a young lady who just now stuck her head out of this door, apparently in need of an umbrella. She is the one I am looking for, I and my umbrella."—You are laughing.—Perhaps you will permit me to send my servant to fetch it tomorrow, or would you rather have me summon a cab? You owe me no thanks, it is only a simple courtesy.—She is certainly one of the gayest maidens I have seen in a long time, her glance is so childlike and yet so saucy, her nature is so charming, so proper, and yet she is curious.—Go in peace, my child, if it weren't for a certain green cloak, I could have wished to get better acquainted. —She walks down Store Kjøbmagergade. How guileless and trusting she was, not a trace of prudery. See how lightly she walks, how pertly she tosses her head! The green cloak demands self-denial.

Thank you, benevolent chance, accept my thanks! Straight was she and proud, mysterious and rich in thought like a spruce tree, a shoot, a thought, which from the depths of the earth shoots up toward the sky, unexplained, inexplicable to itself, a whole without parts. The beech tree develops a crown, its leaves tell us about what has happened beneath it, but the spruce has no crown, no story, it is a mystery to itself—she was like that. She was hidden to herself within herself, she rose up out of herself, there was in her a serene pride like the bold upward surge of the spruce, even though it is rooted in the earth. She had an aura of melancholy like the plaintive cooing of the stock dove, a deep longing which wanted nothing. A riddle was she, who mysteriously possessed the solution to it, a secret—and what are all the secrets of the diplomats in comparison with it, a riddle—and what in all the world is so beautiful as the word that solves it? How significant, how pregnant language is: *at løse,** what an ambiguity the word contains, how beautifully and strongly this ambiguity flows through all the combinations in which the word occurs! Just as the soul's wealth is a riddle as long as the tongue is not loosed, whereby the riddle would be solved, so, too, a young girl is a riddle.

Thanks, benevolent chance, accept my thanks! If I had got to see her in winter, she would have been wrapped up in the

* The Danish verb at *løse* means "to loose" as well as "to solve." Hence both "loosed" and "solved" translate the past participle *løst.*

green cloak, chilled through perhaps, and the harshness of nature would have diminished its own beauty in her. But now, what good fortune is mine! I got to see her for the first time in the most beautiful part of the year, in spring, in the light of the afternoon. To be sure, winter also has its advantages. A brilliantly lighted ballroom can indeed be a flattering setting for a young girl in an evening gown, but she seldom appears to the best advantage here, partly because she is expected to do just that, and this expectation has a disturbing effect on her, whether she gives way or offers resistance to it, and partly because everything here suggests transitoriness and vanity and calls forth an impatience that makes the enjoyment less refreshing. At certain times I should not care to do without the ballroom, I should not care to do without its cherished luxury, its priceless abundance of youth and beauty, its manifold play of forces, but on these occasions I do not enjoy so much as I revel in possibilities. It is not an individual beauty that fascinates me, but a totality. A dream vision floats by, wherein all these feminine beings mingle in a dance figure, as it were, and all these movements seek something, seek rest in *one* image which is not visible.

It was about half past six, on the path that runs between Nørreport and Østerport, the old city gates. The sun had lost its vigor, only the memory of it lingered in a mild glow which spread over the landscape. Nature breathed more freely. The pond was calm, smooth as a mirror. The pleasant houses on the Blegdam were reflected in the water, which farther out was as dark as metal. The path and the buildings on the other side were lighted up by feeble sunrays. The sky was clear and pure, only a single light cloud glided unnoticed across it, best seen by fixing one's eyes on the pond, beyond whose smooth surface it vanished from sight. Not a leaf stirred.

It was she! My eyes did not deceive me, even if the green cloak has done so. Although I had been prepared a long time for this moment, I still found it impossible to control a certain

agitation, a rising and falling like the song of the lark that rose
and fell above the adjacent fields. She was alone. How she was
dressed I have again forgotten, and yet now I have a picture of
her. She was alone, preoccupied not with herself, apparently,
but with her thoughts. She was not thinking, but the quiet play
of her thoughts wove a picture of yearning before her soul, a
picture which was full of presentiment, vague like a young
girl's many sighs. She was at the loveliest period of her life. A
young girl does not develop in the same sense as a boy; she
does not grow, she is born. A boy begins to develop at once
and takes a long time in doing so; a young girl takes a long
time in being born and is born full-grown. Hence her infinite
richness. At the moment of her birth she is full-grown, but this
moment of birth comes late. Therefore she is born twice, the
second time when she marries, or to be more exact: at this
moment she ceases to be born, not until this moment is she
born. It is not only Minerva who springs full-grown from Jupiter's head, not only Venus who rises up from the sea in all
her beauty; like this is every young girl whose womanliness
has not been destroyed by what is called development. She does
not awaken in successive stages, but all at once; on the contrary, she dreams all the longer, provided people are not so
foolish as to arouse her too early. But this dreaming is infinite
richness.

   She was preoccupied not with herself but in herself, and
this preoccupation indicated that infinite peace and rest dwelt
within her. Thus is a young girl rich, and to embrace this richness makes one rich as well. She is rich, although she does not
know that she owns anything: she is rich, she is a treasure.
Quiet peace rested upon her, and gentle melancholy. She was
light to behold, as light as Psyche who is carried away by genii,
even lighter, for she carried herself away. Let the theologians
argue about the assumption of the Madonna; it does not seem
incomprehensible to me, for she no longer belonged to the

world. But a young girl's lightness is incomprehensible and mocks the law of gravity.

She noticed nothing and therefore believed herself unnoticed. I followed at a distance and absorbed her image. She walked slowly, no haste disturbed her peace or the calm of her surroundings. By the pond sat a boy fishing. She stopped to gaze at the water's mirror and the small float. Although she had not walked rapidly, she wanted to cool off and therefore loosened the little kerchief that was fastened about her neck under her shawl. A soft breeze from the pond caressed her bosom, white as snow, and yet warm and full. The boy did not seem to relish having a spectator, he turned around and gave her a rather phlegmatic glance. He really cut a ridiculous figure, and I cannot hold it against her that she began to laugh at him. How youthfully she laughed! Had she been alone with the boy, I do not believe that she would have been afraid to fight with him. Her eyes were large and radiant; when one gazed into them, they had a dark luster that gave one a feeling of infinite depth, impossible to fathom. They were pure and innocent, gentle and calm, but full of mischief when she smiled. Her nose was delicately arched. When I saw her profile, her nose merged into her forehead, which made it look a little shorter, a little saucier.

She walked on and I followed. Fortunately there were several strollers on the path. While I exchanged a few words with one and another of these, I let her gain a little on me and then quickly caught up with her again, thus relieving myself of the necessity of walking as slowly as she did while following her at a distance. She was strolling in the direction of Østerport. I was anxious to see her at a closer range without being seen. At the corner there is a house from which I should be able to do so. I know the family that lives there and needed no excuse to pay it a call. I hurried past the girl with rapid steps as if I were not paying her the slightest attention. I managed to put a considerable distance between us, greeted the family effusively, and then took possession of the window overlooking the path. She came, I looked and looked, engaged at the same time in a conversation with the tea party in the drawing room. Her walk easily convinced me that she had not attended dancing school for any length of time, and yet there was a pride in it, a natural nobility, but also a lack of preoccupation with her person. I got to see her one more time than I had expected. From the window my eyes could not follow the path very far, but I was able to see a pier extending out into the pond, and to my great surprise I caught sight of her out there. It occurred to me that perhaps she lived out here in the country, perhaps her family had a summer home here.

I was about to regret my visit for fear that she might turn back and I lose sight of her; yes, the very circumstance that she became visible out there at the far end of the pier was, as it were, a sign that I was losing her. But then she suddenly reappeared close by. She had already passed the house. Quickly I snatched up my hat and cane in the hope that I might be able to pass her and fall back a number of times until I had discovered her abode, but in my haste I jostled the arm of a lady who was serving tea. A terrible outcry arose. I stood there with my hat and cane, intent solely on getting away, and in order to manage my escape and motivate my retreat, I uttered in a voice full of pathos, "Let me be banished like Cain from this place, which witnessed the spilling of this tea!" But as if everything had conspired against me, the host conceived the desperate idea of following up my remark by declaring solemnly that I should not be allowed to go until I had enjoyed a cup of tea and had set everything right again by serving the ladies whose tea I had spilled. Since I was convinced that in the present circumstances the host would regard it as an act of politeness to resort to force, there was nothing for me to do but to remain.

She had vanished!

How beautiful it is to be in love, how interesting it is to know that one is in love. Behold, that is the difference! I can grow bitter at the thought that for a second time she has escaped me, and yet in a certain sense it pleases me. The image I possess of her shifts uncertainly between her actual and her ideal form. This image I now summon before me, but it has a peculiar magic for the very reason that it either is reality or the reality is the occasion.

I do not feel impatient, for I now know that she lives here in the city, and at present that is enough for me. Because of this likelihood her image may be evoked vividly—everything should be savored in slow draughts. And should I not be content, I who may regard myself as a favorite of the gods, who had the rare good fortune to fall in love again? That, after all, is something no art, no study can effect, it is a gift. But if I have been fortunate enough to enjoy the state of love again, I wish to find out how long it may be sustained. I pamper this love as I never did my first. The opportunity befalls one rarely enough; if it does appear, it is, to be sure, vitally important to seize it. For this is the desperate truth of the matter: it requires no art to seduce a girl, but good fortune is needed to find one worth seducing.

Love has many mysteries, and falling in love for the first time is also a mystery, albeit a minor one. Most people rush forward, become engaged or commit some other foolishness, and in the twinkling of an eye it is all over, and they do not know what they have won or what they have lost. Twice now she has appeared before me and vanished; that means that soon she will appear more frequently. When Joseph explained Pharaoh's dream, he added, "And the fact that thou didst dream this twice, signifies that it will soon be fulfilled."

It would indeed be interesting if we could see a little in advance the forces whose appearance constitutes life's content. She lives now in all her calm peace; she does not yet suspect that I exist, still less the certainty with which I gaze into her future; for my soul demands reality more and more, it grows stronger and stronger. When a girl at first sight does not produce such a deep impression upon one that she awakens the ideal, then the reality is generally not especially desirable; if, on the contrary, she does awaken the ideal, one is usually somewhat overwhelmed, no matter how experienced one may be. I always advise the person who is not certain of his hand, his eye, and his victory to risk the attack in this first condition, in which he has supernatural powers for the very reason that he is overwhelmed; for this state of being overwhelmed is a curious blending of affection and egoism. His enjoyment, however, will be impaired; for he is too much involved in the situation, too much absorbed by it, to be able to enjoy it. What is the most beautiful is difficult to decide, what is the most interesting is easy to decide. However, it is always advisable to come as close as possible to the dividing line. This affords the real enjoyment; what others may enjoy I am unable to say. Mere possession is very little, and the means which such lovers employ are usually wretched enough. They do not disdain the employment of money, power, the influence of others, soporifics, and so on. But what enjoyment can there be in love if it lacks absolute surrender, that is, on one side? But such surrender as a rule requires spirit, and this is what these lovers as a rule lack.

So her name is Cordelia. Cordelia! It is a lovely name. This,, too, is important, as it is often upsetting to have to use the most tender epithets in connection with an ugly name. I recognized her from afar, she was walking with two other girls on her left. The way they walked seemed to indicate that they would soon stop. I stood at the street corner and read a poster, all the time keeping an eye on my unknown one. They took leave of one another. The two apparently had gone a little out of their way, for they now retraced their steps in the opposite direction. She walked on toward my street corner. When she had taken a few steps, one of the young girls came running after her, calling loudly enough for me to hear, "Cordelia! Cordelia!" Then the third girl joined them and they put their heads together in a secret conference, the import of which I tried in vain to overhear. Then all three laughed, and at a somewhat accelerated pace they hurried back in the direction the two had taken before. I followed them. They entered a house on the Strand. I waited for a while, since it seemed likely that Cordelia would soon return alone. But this did not happen.

Cordelia! It is an excellent name indeed, it was the name of King Lear's third daughter, that remarkable girl who did not heave her heart into her mouth, whose lips were silent while her heart swelled with feeling. So it is with my Cordelia. She resembles her, of that I am certain. And yet in another sense her heart does dwell on her lips, not in the form of words, but more heartily in the form of a kiss. How swelling with health her lips were! Never have I seen more beautiful ones.

That I am really in love I can tell among other things by the secretiveness with which I treat this matter, even to myself. All love is secretive, even the faithless kind, provided it has within itself the proper aesthetic moment. It has never occurred to me to desire confidants or to boast of my adventures. I am therefore almost glad that I did not find out where her home is, but only a place she frequently visits. Perhaps because of this I have even come a little closer to my goal. I can make my observations without attracting her attention, and from this fixed point I shall not find it difficult to gain access to her family. Should this circumstance, on the contrary, prove to be a difficulty—*eh bien!* I shall take it in my stride. Everything I do, I do *con amore;* and so I also love *con amore.*

Today I managed to obtain some information about the house into which she disappeared. It is inhabited by a widow with three fine daughters. There is plenty of information to be had here, that is to say, information within certain limits. The only difficulty is in comprehending this information when raised to the third power, for all three of them talk at the same time. Her name is Cordelia Wahl, and she is the daughter of a Navy captain. He died several years ago; her mother is also dead. He was a very hard, strict man. She now lives with her aunt, her father's sister, who is said to be like her brother, but who otherwise is a very respectable woman. This is all very nice, but for the rest they know nothing about the aunt's house. They never go there, but Cordelia often comes to their place. She and the two girls are learning the culinary art in the Royal Kitchen. She therefore usually visits them early in the afternoon, sometimes in the forenoon, never in the evening. They live in a very retired manner.

Thus ends their account. There is no suggestion of a bridge over which I might slip into Cordelia's house.

She has, then, some comprehension of life's sorrows and of its dark side. Who would have imagined that? But no doubt these memories belong to her earlier years, they form a horizon under which she has lived without really being aware of it.

This is all to the good, it has saved her womanliness, she has not been spoiled. On the other hand, it will also be important in raising her to a higher level, provided one really understands how to bring it out. All such matters usually generate pride if they do not crush, and she is indeed far from being crushed.

the 21st.

She lives near the Rampart. The location is not very favorable as far as I am concerned; on the opposite side there are no neighbors whose acquaintance one might make, and there are no public places where one might carry on observations unnoticed. The Rampart itself is little suitable, one is too exposed. If one strolls along the street below, one cannot very well walk on the side of the Rampart, for no one goes there and it would attract undue attention, but if one walks on the side where the houses are, one can see nothing. It is a corner house. The windows facing the courtyard can also be seen from the street, as there is no neighboring house. Her bedroom is probably on that side.

the 22nd.

Today I saw her for the first time at Mrs. Jansen's. I was introduced to her. She didn't seem to be particularly interested in
the introduction or in me. I kept in the background as much
as possible in order to observe her the better. She stayed only
a moment, having come for the daughters on her way to the
cooking course. While the Jansen girls were putting on their
things, we two were alone in the living-room. In a cold, almost
insultingly casual manner I uttered a few words, which she answered with undeserved courtesy. Then they left. I could have
offered to accompany them, but that would have sufficed to
stamp me as a gallant, and I am convinced that she is not to
be won that way. I preferred to leave directly after her departure, but I walked much more rapidly than they and along
other streets likewise leading to the Royal Kitchen, so that just
as they were about to turn into Store Kongensgade, I dashed
past them without even a word of greeting or a nod, to their
great astonishment.

the 23rd.

It is essential that I gain entrance to her home; in military par-
lance, I am ready for action. It promises, however, to be an
involved and arduous task. I have never known a family living
in such seclusion. There are only herself and her aunt. No
brothers, no cousins, not a thread to take hold of, no ever so
distant relatives with whom one might lock arms. I constantly
go about with one arm hanging free. Not for anything in the
world would I go arm in arm with someone on either side. My
arm is a grappling iron always kept in readiness, intended for
unexpected developments, in case there should appear in the
distance a far removed relative or a friend whom I might reach
out for and take by the arm—and thus climb on board.

Anyway, it is wrong for a family to live so isolated; the poor
girl is deprived of the opportunity to get to know the world,
to say nothing of other dangerous consequences. This sort of
thing is always self-defeating. The same is true of courting. No
doubt such isolation offers protection against petty thieves.
In a house with much social life opportunity makes the thief,
but that is hardly very important. From such girls there is
not much to steal; when they are sixteen years old, their
hearts already are like samplers embroidered all over with
names, and I don't care to write my name where several
already have written theirs. I never feel the urge to scratch my
name on a window pane or in an inn or on a tree or a bench
in Frederiksberg Park.

The more I observe her, the more I am convinced that she is a very isolated figure. A man ought never to be so, not even a youth, for since his development essentially depends upon reflection, he must have entered into relation with others. A young girl must therefore not be interesting, for the interesting always contains a reflection upon itself; therefore in art the most interesting always reflects the artist. A young girl who wishes to please by being interesting really seeks to please herself. This is the objection from the aesthetic side to all kinds of coquetry. The case is quite different when it comes to that figurative coquetry which is an expression of nature, as for instance feminine modesty, which is coquetry at its most beautiful.

An interesting girl may be able to please, but just as she herself has given up her femininity, so also the men she pleases usually are unmanly ones. Such a young girl really becomes interesting only through her relationship to men. Woman is the weaker sex, and yet it is far more essential for her to be alone in her youth than for a man; she must be self-contained, but that through which and in which she is self-contained is an illusion. This illusion is the dowry nature has endowed her with, as if she were a king's daughter. But this resting in illusion is just what isolates her. I have often wondered why it is that there is nothing more corrupting for a young girl than constant association with other young girls. The reason evidently is that this association is neither one thing nor the other: it disturbs the illusion, but it does not explain it. Woman's profoundest destiny is to be company for man, but through association with her own sex a reflection is easily drawn to it which makes of her a lady's companion instead of company. The language itself is highly significant in this respect: man is called master, but woman is not called maidservant or the like; no, a category of the essential is used: she is company, not female companion.

If I were to imagine the ideal girl, it would be a girl who is always alone in the world, who thereby is self-contained, and who above everything else has no girl friends. To be sure, the Graces were three in number, but surely it has never occurred to anyone to imagine them talking together; in their silent trinity they form a beautiful feminine unity. In this respect I would be inclined to advise reviving ladies' bowers, if such confinement were not also harmful. It is always highly desirable that a young girl be granted freedom, but that no opportunities be offered her. Thus she becomes beautiful and is protected from becoming interesting. A young girl who spends much time in the company of young girls is given a bridal veil in vain. In contrast, a man with sufficient aesthetic appreciation always finds that a girl who is innocent in the truest sense comes to him veiled, even if it is not the custom to wear a bridal veil.

She has been strictly brought up; for this I honor her parents in their graves. She lives in a very secluded manner; for this I could embrace her aunt in gratitude. She has not learned to know the pleasures of the world, she is not flightily blasée. She is proud, she scorns that which other young girls cherish, and this is as it should be. It is a paradox of which I shall be able to take advantage. Splendor and display do not please her in the same sense as they please other young girls; she is a little polemical, but this is necessary for a young girl with her feelings. She lives in a world of fantasy. If she were to fall into the wrong hands, something very unfeminine might be developed in her for the very reason that she is so very feminine.

Everywhere our paths cross. Today I met her three times. I know all her comings and goings, I know when and where I can meet her, but this knowledge is not used to bring about a meeting with her. On the contrary, I squander my opportunities on a frightfully lavish scale. An encounter which has cost me several hours of waiting is squandered as if it were a bagatelle. I do not meet her, I merely touch the periphery of her existence. If I know that she is going to Mrs. Jansen's, I am not anxious to meet her there, unless it is important for me to make some special observation. I prefer to arrive at Mrs. Jansen's shortly before she turns up and then to meet her, if possible, at the door, as she comes in, or on the stairs, where I casually hurry past her. This is the first net in which she must be entangled. On the street I never stop her, or if we do exchange greetings, I never come close to her, but always keep my distance. She cannot help noticing our frequent encounters, she is indeed aware that on her horizon a new body has appeared, whose orbit in a strangely unobtrusive manner interferes obtrusively with her own orbit. But she has no conception of the law constituting this movement; rather is she inclined to look about her, to the right and to the left, to see if she can discover the point which represents the center of attraction. She realizes as little as her own antipode that she is this center of attraction. It is with her as it is with my acquaintances in general: they believe that I have a multiplicity of

affairs, that I am constantly on the move, that I say like
Figaro, "One, two, three, four intrigues at the same time, that
is my joy."

I must know her and her entire intellectual condition before
I begin my attack. Most men enjoy a young girl the way they
enjoy a glass of champagne, in one spumescent moment. Ah
yes, that is quite pleasant, and in the case of many young girls
it probably is the most one can attain, but here there is more.
If the individual is too weak to bear clearness and transpar-
ency, then one enjoys what is unclear, but she can evidently
bear it. The more one can abandon oneself to love, the
more interesting. This enjoyment of the moment is, if not in a
physical, then in a figurative sense, a ravishment, and in a
ravishment there is only imagined enjoyment; it is like a stolen
kiss, something which is a substitute. No, when one can bring
it about that a girl sees in the abandonment of her self the sole
purpose of her freedom, that she feels her whole happiness depends on this abandonment, that she does not shrink from ob-
taining it by begging and yet is free, then and only then is
there enjoyment. But this always requires intellectual influence.

Cordelia! A glorious name indeed! I sit at home and practice
talking like a parrot, I say, "Cordelia, Cordelia, my Cordelia,
my own Cordelia." I cannot refrain from smiling at the thought
of the routine with which I shall utter these words when the
decisive moment comes. One should always make preliminary
studies, everything should be prepared just so. It is no wonder
that the poets never fail to describe the beautiful moment
when lovers first call each other by their Christian names, the
intimate moment when they divest themselves of the old being,
not by sprinkling (to be sure, there are many who never get
any further than that), but by descending into the waters of
love, from which they rise as from a baptism, and for the first
time really know each other like old friends, although they are
but a moment old. For a young girl this moment is always the
most beautiful, and in order to enjoy it rightly, one ought al-

ways to be a little above it, so as to be not only the person to be baptized but also the baptizer. A bit of irony makes this moment's next moment one of the most interesting, it is a spiritual disrobing. One must be poet enough not to disturb the ceremony, and yet the rogue in one must always be lying in wait.

June 2nd.

She is proud, I have seen that for a long time. When she is together with the Jansens, she says very little, their chatter obviously bores her, a certain smile about her lips seems to indicate it. On this smile I am building. At other times she abandons herself to an almost boyish wildness, to the great surprise of the Jansens. It is not inexplicable to me when I consider her childhood. She had only one brother, who was a year older. The only men she has known were her father and brother; she has witnessed grave scenes, which developed in her a distaste for chitchat in general. Her father and mother did not live happily together; that which usually attracts a young girl more or less clearly or vaguely does not attract her. It may very well be that she is puzzled about what it means to be a woman. Perhaps there are moments when she wishes she were a man instead of a woman.

She has imagination, a soul, passion, in short, all the substantialities, but not subjectively reflected. I found that out by chance today. I know from the Jansen company that she does not play a musical instrument, as this is against her aunt's principles. I have always regretted this, for music is a good means of establishing communication with a young girl, provided one is cautious enough not to pose as a connoisseur.

Today I again went up to Mrs. Jansen's. I had half opened the door without knocking—a rudeness on my part that has often served me well and which, when necessary, I try to mitigate by the absurd action of tapping on the open door—when

57

I saw her sitting alone at the piano. She seemed to be playing furtively. It was a little Swedish melody. She did not play with skill, she became impatient, but then softer tones were produced. I closed the door and stood outside, listening to the changes in her moods. At times there was an intensity in her playing which reminded one of the maiden Mettelil, who smote the golden harp so that milk gushed from her breasts. There was something melancholic but also something dithyrambic in her performance. I might have rushed in and seized the moment, but that would have been folly.

Memory is not only a means of preserving, it is also a means of enhancing; what is suffused with memory has a two-fold effect. One often finds in books, especially in hymnals, a little flower: a beautiful moment furnished the occasion for placing it there, but the memory is even more beautiful. She is obviously trying to hide the fact that she knows how to play, or perhaps she plays only this little Swedish melody. Has it perhaps a special interest for her? All this I do not know, but therefore this incident is of great importance to me. When on some future occasion I shall converse more confidentially with her, I shall slyly guide her to this point and let her fall into the trap.

June 3rd.

I am still unable to decide how she is to be understood. Therefore I keep very quiet, very inconspicuous, like a soldier on vedette duty who flings himself on the ground and listens for the faintest echo indicating an approaching enemy. I really do not exist for her, not in the sense of a negative relationship, rather in the sense of no relationship at all. So far I have not dared to experiment.—To see her was to love her, thus they say in novels. Yes, it is true enough, if love had no dialectic, but what, after all, does one learn about love from novels? Nothing but lies, which help to shorten the task.

When after the information I have obtained I think back upon the impression that first meeting made on me, my ideas are modified, it is true, but to her advantage as well as to mine. It is not exactly an everyday occurrence that a young girl walks about all alone or that a young girl is so self-absorbed. She was subjected to my strict appraisal: charming. But charm is a very transient stage, which vanishes and is gone as completely as yesterday. I had not imagined her in the surroundings in which she lives; least of all had I imagined her so unreflectively familiar with life's storms.

I would like to know the state of her emotional life. Surely she has never been in love, for the flight of her spirit is too free for that; least of all does she belong to those theoretically experienced maidens who, long before their time, are accustomed to imagine themselves in the arms of the man they love. The real-life figures she has met have not been able to render her confused about the relation of dream and reality. Her soul is still nourished by the divine ambrosia of ideals. But the ideal which hovers before her is not exactly a shepherdess or a heroine in a novel, a mistress, but rather someone like Jeanne d'Arc.

The question will always be whether her femininity is strong enough to let it reflect itself or whether it is to be enjoyed only as beauty and charm; the question is whether one dares to draw the bow more tightly. It is already something wonderful to find a pure immediate femininity, but if one dares to attempt the change, then one gets the interesting. In such a case it is best to provide her with an ordinary suitor. That this would be harmful for a young girl is nothing but a popular superstition.—Yes, if she is a very fine and sensitive plant with but one outstanding attraction, namely charm, it is indeed best for her never to have heard of love, but if this is not the case, then it is an advantage, and I should never hesitate to provide her with a suitor, if none were available. This suitor must not be a caricature either, for then nothing is gained; he must be a highly respectable young man, even attractive if possible, but inadequate for her passion. She looks down on such a man, she develops a distaste for love, she nearly despairs of her own reality when she feels her destiny and sees what reality offers. If this is all there is to love, she says, then what is all the shouting about? She grows proud in her love, this pride makes her interesting, it radiates her being with a higher incarnation. At the same time, however, she approaches her downfall, but all this only makes her more and more interesting. Still, it is best first to find out about her acquaintances to see whether there is such a suitor among them. Her home offers no opportunity, for almost nobody visits there, but she does go out, and so she may indeed find such a one. To provide a suitor before knowing this is always a risky undertaking; two suitors, each of whom is insignificant, could have a harmful effect because of their relativity. I must find out whether such a lover is not hiding somewhere, one who lacks the courage to storm the citadel, a chicken thief, who sees no opportunity in such a convent-like house.

The strategic principle, the law governing all moves in this campaign, will therefore be always to involve her in an interesting situation. The interesting, then, is the terrain on which the battle must be waged, the potentialities of the interesting must be exhausted. Unless I am very much mistaken, her whole being is designed for this, so that what I ask for is exactly what she gives, indeed, what she herself asks for. The important thing is to find out what the individual can give and what she consequently demands. For this reason my love affairs always have a reality for myself, they constitute stages, creative periods in my life, of which I am fully aware; often they are even associated with one or another acquired skill. Thus I learned to dance for the sake of the first girl I loved, I learned to speak French for the sake of a little dancer. In those days, like all ninnies, I went to the market place and was often made a fool of. Now I go in for illegal traffic. Perhaps, however, she has exhausted one side of the interesting; her secluded life would indicate that. It is important, therefore, to find another side, which at first sight may not seem interesting to her, but which may become so just because of this objection. For this purpose I select not the poetic but the prosaic. This, then, is the beginning. At first her femininity is neutralized by prosaic good sense and ridicule, not directly but indirectly, as well as by the absolutely neutral, by the intellect. She nearly loses her sense of femininity, but in this condition she cannot remain alone, she throws herself into my arms, not as if I were a lover, no, still in a completely neutral manner. Then her femininity awakens, all its potentialities are evoked, she is induced to give offense to one or another convention, she rises above it, her femininity reaches nearly supernatural heights, and she belongs to me with a world-passion.

I did not have to go far. She sometimes is a guest in the house of a wholesale merchant, Baxter by name. Here I found not only her, but also a man whose presence proved most opportune. Edvard, the son of the house, is head over heels in love with her. One needs but to look at his two eyes with half an eye to realize that. He works in his father's office and is a good-looking fellow, quite pleasant, somewhat bashful, which last I think does him no harm as far as she is concerned.

Poor Edvard! He simply does not know what to do with his love. When he knows that she will be present in the evening, he dresses carefully for her sake alone, puts on his new black suit for her sake alone, wears cuffs for her sake alone, and cuts an almost ridiculous figure among the otherwise quite commonplace company in the drawing room. His embarrassment borders on the incredible. If this were a mask, Edvard would become a dangerous rival for me. It requires great art to make effective use of embarrassment, but one can obtain a great deal with it. How often have I not used embarrassment to fool some little maiden! Generally girls speak very disparagingly about bashful men, and yet secretly they are rather fond of them. A little embarrassment flatters such a girl's vanity, she is conscious of her superiority, it is earnest money. When one has lulled them to sleep, when they are inclined to believe that one is ready to die from embarrassment, then one shows them that one is very far from doing that and is quite able to go one's way alone. By means of embarrassment one loses one's masculine significance, and it is therefore a relatively good means of neutralizing the sexual relationship. Consequently they feel ashamed when they notice that it was only a mask, they blush inwardly, they feel very strongly that in a way they have exceeded their bounds. It is just as if they continue too long to treat a boy as a child.

And so we are friends now, Edvard and I. It is a true friendship, a beautiful relationship, such as has not existed since the most glorious days of ancient Greece. We soon became confidants when, after having involved him in an abundance of reflections about Cordelia, I got him to confess his secret. It goes without saying that when all secrets are being assembled, this one is revealed with the rest. Poor chap, he has been sighing for a long time. He dresses up each time she comes, he accompanies her home in the evening, his heart beats faster at the mere thought of her arm resting on his, they gaze at the stars, he rings her doorbell, she disappears, he despairs, but keeps on hoping. Despite such excellent opportunities he has not yet had the courage to cross her threshold. Although inwardly I cannot help making fun of Edvard, it cannot be denied that there is something touchingly beautiful in his childishness. Although I like to imagine that I am fairly well versed in the entire gamut of the erotic, I must admit that I have never observed this condition in myself, this fear and trembling from being in love, that is, never to the degree that it deprives me of my self-possession. Actually I do know this condition, but on me it has the effect that it only makes me stronger. Perhaps some will say that I have never really been in love. Perhaps.

After having taken Edvard to task, I encouraged him to depend on my friendship. Tomorrow he will take a decisive step, he will go to her house and invite her. I drew him on to the desperate idea of asking me to accompany him, which I then promised to do. He regards this as an extraordinary expression of friendship on my part. The occasion is exactly as I would have it: we shall take the citadel by surprise. Should she have the faintest doubt as to the meaning of my appearing there, my appearance itself will confuse everything.

Formerly I never used to prepare myself for my part in a conversation, but now this has become a necessity for me in order to entertain the aunt. I have assumed the honorable task of conversing with the aunt in order to cover Edvard's amorous tactics with regard to Cordelia. The aunt formerly lived in the country, and because of my own thorough studies in the field of agricultural literature and the aunt's statements based on experience I am making considerable progress in insight and efficiency.

I am completely successful with the aunt, she regards me as a sedate and steady person whom it is a pleasure to entertain and who is not like our dandies. I do not seem to have made a very favorable impression on Cordelia. To be sure, her femininity is too pure and innocent for her to demand that every man dance attendance upon her, but still she is very conscious of the rebellious element in my nature.

When I sit thus in the comfortable living room, when she like a good angel spreads charm everywhere, over everyone with whom she comes in contact, over good and evil, then I sometimes become inwardly impatient and I am tempted to rush forward from my hiding place. The reason is that although I sit there, visible to everyone in the living room, I am really lying in ambush. I am tempted to grasp her hand, to take all of her in my arms, to hide her within me, lest anyone should deprive me of her. Or when Edvard and I leave in the evening and she offers me her hand in parting, when I hold it in mine, then I sometimes find it difficult to let the bird slip out of my hand. Patience! *Quod antea fuit impetus, nunc ratio est* [What before was an urge, now is method]. She

must be drawn quite otherwise into my web, and then I
shall suddenly let the whole power of love rush forth. We have
not spoiled that moment for ourselves by sampling, by unseemly anticipation, you can thank me for that, my Cordelia. I
work to develop the contrast, I tauten the bow of love to
wound the deeper. Like an archer, I release the string, tighten
it again, listen to its song, which is my battle music, but still I
do not aim, still I do not lay the arrow on the string.

When a small number of people frequently gather in the
same room, then a convention is easily developed as to where
each person has his own place, and a picture is formed which
each one can reproduce for himself at will, a chart of the terrain. Such a picture we now form in the Wahl home. In the evening we drink tea there. Generally the aunt, who till then has
been sitting on the sofa, moves over to the small sewing table,
which place in turn is vacated by Cordelia, who betakes herself to the tea table in front of the sofa. Edvard follows her to
the sofa, and I follow the aunt. Edvard seeks secretiveness,
he wants to whisper, and he usually does this so well that he
ends up by being entirely mute. I make no secret of my out-
pourings to the aunt—market prices, an estimate of the number of liters of milk needed to produce a pound of butter, and
on through the medium of cream and the dialectic of the butter churn: not only are these subjects any young girl can
safely listen to but they also provide the elements of a solid,
profound, and edifying conversation, equally improving for
mind and heart. I generally turn my back to the tea table and
to Edvard's and Cordelia's gushing. In the meantime I gush
with the aunt. And is not nature great and wise in her prod-
ucts, what a precious gift butter is, what a glorious result of
nature and art! I had promised Edvard to prevent the aunt
from overhearing the conversation between him and Cordelia, provided anything was really said, and I always keep
my word. I, on the other hand, can easily overhear every word
they exchange, hear every movement. This is of great impor-

tance to me, for one cannot know how far a desperate man will dare to go. The most cautious and pusillanimous men sometimes dare the most desperate things. Although I have nothing at all to do with these two isolated people, it is apparent to me that Cordelia feels that I am constantly, albeit invisibly, present between her and Edvard.

We four together compose a peculiar picture indeed. I could find an analogy in the realm of familiar paintings in so far as I think of myself as Mephistopheles; the difficulty here is that Edvard is no Faust. If I take the part of Faust, then the new difficulty arises that Edvard is no Mephistopheles. Neither am I a Mephistopheles, least of all in Edvard's eyes. He regards me as the good genius of his love, and he is right in that, at least he can be certain that no one can watch more solicitously over his love than I. I have promised him to converse with the aunt, and I carry out this honorable task with all seriousness. The aunt nearly vanishes before our eyes into the realm of purely agricultural matters. We go down into the kitchen and the cellars, we go up into the attic, we look after the chickens, ducks, and geese, and so on. All this annoys Cordelia. Of course she cannot understand what I really want. I become a riddle to her, a riddle she is not tempted to solve, but which vexes her and even makes her indignant. She feels very keenly that her aunt is making herself more or less ridiculous, and yet her aunt is a highly respectable lady who certainly does not deserve such treatment. On the other hand, I manage everything so adroitly that she knows very well that any attempt on her part to depose me would be futile. Sometimes I carry things so far that I induce Cordelia to smile secretly about her aunt. These are studies that must be made. Not as if I did this in union with Cordelia; by no means, in that case I would never get her to smile about her aunt. I continue to be unvaryingly serious and thorough, but she cannot refrain from smiling. It is the first falsity she must be taught: to smile ironically; but this smile is directed at me almost as much as at her aunt, for she simply does not know what to think of me. It is just possible that I am one of those prematurely old young men, it is possible; there is also a second possibility, a third one, and so on. When she has smiled about the aunt, she is angry with herself. I turn around, and while I continue to converse with the aunt, I look at her very seriously, and then she smiles about me and about the situation.

Our relationship is not the tender and loyal embrace of understanding, it is not attraction, it is the repulsion of misunderstanding. My relationship to her is really nothing at all; it is a purely intellectual one, which means that it is nothing at all from a young girl's point of view. Still, the method I now pursue has its extraordinary conveniences. A person who appears on the scene as a gallant awakens mistrust and meets with resistance. From all this I am exempt. One does not keep an eye on me; on the contrary, one is inclined to regard me as a trustworthy person who is fit to keep an eye on a young girl. The method has but one drawback: it is slow, but it can therefore be used advantageously against individuals when the interesting is to be gained.

What a rejuvenating power a young girl has! Not the freshness of a morning breeze, not the soughing of the wind, not the sea's coolness, not the wine's aroma, nor its deliciousness— nothing else in the world has this rejuvenating power.

I hope that soon I shall have brought her to the point of hating me. I play the part of a bachelor to perfection. I talk of nothing but sitting cosily, lying comfortably, having a reliable servant, a friend whose feet are firmly planted on the ground, so that one can depend on him when one walks arm in arm with him. Whenever I can induce the aunt to give up the agricultural discussions, I lead her to these matters in order to get a more direct occasion for irony. One can laugh at a bachelor, yes, one can even feel a little pity for him, but a young man who is not without intellect arouses the indigna-

tion of a young girl with such conduct; the entire significance
of her sex, its beauty, and its poetry are destroyed.

So the days elapse, I see her, but I do not talk with her, I
talk with the aunt in her presence. Occasionally at night it may
occur to me to give my feelings of love an airing. Then,
wrapped in my cloak, with my cap pulled down over my eyes,
I walk up and down in front of her windows. Her bedroom
overlooks the courtyard, but since it is a corner house, it can
be seen from the street. Sometimes she stands a moment at the
window, or she opens it and looks up at the stars, unseen by
all except the one she would least of all believe was watching
her. In these hours of the night I go about like an apparition,
like an apparition I frequent the place where her house is.
Then I forget everything, I have no plans, no calculations, I
cast reason overboard, I expand and strengthen my breast with
deep sighs, an exercise I need in order not to suffer from the
routinized character of my life. Some are virtuous by day and
sin at night; I am dissimulation by day, at night I am all
desire. If she saw me here, if she could peer into my soul—if!

If this girl wants to understand herself, she must admit that
I am the man for her. She is too intense, too deeply moved to
find happiness in marriage; it would be too little for her to
succumb to an ordinary seducer; if she succumbs to me, then
she will save the interesting out of this shipwreck. In relation
to me she must, as the philosophers say with a play on words,
zu Grunde gehen [founder].

She is really weary of listening to Edvard. It is always like
that: where narrow limits are set for the interesting, one discovers all the more. At times she listens to my conversation
with her aunt. When I notice this, there comes an intimation
from a wholly different world, flashing on the distant horizon,
to the amazement of both the aunt and Cordelia. The aunt sees
the flash, but hears nothing. Cordelia hears the voice, but sees
nothing. In the same moment, however, everything returns to

the old calmness, the conversation between the aunt and me jogs along monotonously, like post horses in the quiet of the night. The melancholy hum of the samovar accompanies it. In such moments there sometimes develops an uncomfortable atmosphere in the living room, especially for Cordelia. She has no one she can talk with or listen to. If she turns to Edvard, she runs the risk of his doing something foolish in his embarrassment; if she turns to the other side, to her aunt and me, then the prevailing certainty, the monotonous hammerblows of our measured conversation, produces the most unpleasant contrast to Edvard's uncertainty.

I can well understand that Cordelia must think the aunt bewitched, so completely does she move in the tempo of my measure. Nor can she participate in this conversation, for one of the means I have adopted to provoke her is that I take the liberty of treating her altogether as a child. Not that I on that account would permit myself any liberties with her, far from it, well I know what an upsetting effect such things can have, and it is particularly important that her womanliness should be able to rise up again pure and beautiful. On account of the intimacy I cultivate with the aunt, it is easy for me to treat her like a child that knows nothing about the world. Thereby her femininity is not offended, but only neutralized, for it cannot offend her femininity that she is ignorant of market prices, but it arouses her indignation that this is supposed to be the ultimate in life. The aunt surpasses herself in this direction with my vigorous support. She has become almost fanatical on the subject, a development she has me to thank for. The only thing she disapproves of in me is that I am nothing. I have therefore made it my custom to exclaim, every time there is talk about a vacant position, "That's a job for me!" and then to discuss it very seriously with her. Cordelia always notices the irony, which is exactly what I want.

Poor Edvard! Too bad his name isn't Fritz. Whenever in my quiet reflections I think of my association with him, I am al-

ways reminded of Fritz in *La Fiancée*. Edvard, like his proto-
type, is a corporal in the militia. To be quite honest, Edvard is
also pretty boring. He does not attack the matter in the right
way, he always turns up looking too natty and prim. Just between ourselves, as a favor to him, I always appear dressed as
carelessly as possible. Poor Edvard! The only thing that almost
makes me feel sorry for him is that he feels so extremely be-
holden to me that he hardly knows how to thank me. To allow
him to thank me for this—it is really too much!

Why can't you be nice and quiet now? All morning you have
been doing nothing but shake my awning, tamper with my
window mirror and its cord, play with the bell-pull from the
fourth story, bump against the windowpanes, in short, an-
nounce your presence in every possible way, as if you would
beckon me to come out with you. Yes, the weather is fine, but
I don't feel like it. Let me stay at home.

You playful, wanton zephyrs, you merry boys, you can very
well go alone; have your fun as always with the girls. Yes, I
know, no one is able to embrace a young girl so seductively as
you; in vain she tries to squirm out of your clasp, she cannot
free herself from your hold—and she doesn't really wish to,
for you are cooling and refreshing, you do not excite her.

Go your own way, do not count on me! You answer that without me you derive no pleasure from your activities, you do not
undertake them for your own sake. Very well, then, I'll go
along, but on two conditions. In the first place. There lives on
Kongens Nytorv a young girl who is very attractive, but she
has the insolence to refuse to love me, and what is even worse,
she loves another, and the situation is so serious that they go
out walking together arm in arm. I know that at one o'clock he
is going to call for her. Now promise me that the strongest
blowers among you will remain in hiding somewhere in the
neighborhood until the moment when he steps out of the house

door with her. At the very moment when he is about to turn down Store Kongensgade, this detachment will rush forward, remove his hat from his head in the politest manner possible and bear it along at an even speed at exactly a yard's distance in front of him; not any faster, for otherwise he might turn back home again. All the time he'll believe he is going to catch it the very next second, and so he won't even let go of her arm. In this way you will conduct them through Store Kongensgade, along the rampart to Nørreport and then to Høibroplads. How much time may this require? I think about half an hour. At half past one exactly, I approach from Østergade. When the detachment concerned has brought the lovers out into the middle of the Place, a violent assault will be made upon them, in the course of which you will also tear her hat from her head, dishevel her locks, and carry away her shawl, while all the time his hat jubilantly rises higher and higher into the air. In short, you will effect a confusion so great that the entire honorable public, not just I alone, will burst into uproarious laughter, the dogs will begin to bark, and the watchman on his tower ring his bell. You will bring it about that her hat flies over to me, who shall have the pleasure of returning it to her.

In the second place. The detachment following me will obey my every signal, it will remain within the bounds of propriety, offer no affront to any pretty girl, and take no liberty that in the course of the jest would prevent her childlike soul from preserving its joy, her lips their smile, her eyes their tranquillity, and her heart its freedom from anxiety. If a single one of you dares to behave differently, your name shall be accursed.

And now away to life and joy, to youth and beauty! Show me what I have often seen, what I never grow tired of seeing, show me a beautiful young maiden, unfold her beauty before me in such a way that she becomes even more beautiful, examine her in such a way that she takes pleasure in that examination!—I choose Bredgade, but, as you know, I can dispose of my time only till half past one.

There comes a young girl in all her finery, this being Sunday . . . Fan her a little, waft coolness in her direction, glide over her in gentle currents, enfold her in your innocent embrace! How I sense the delicate blush of her cheeks, the reddening of her lips, her bosom's rising! It is indescribable, is it not, my girl, it is a blessed delight to inhale this refreshing breeze? The little collar rises and falls like a leaf. How full and sound her breathing is! Her pace slackens, she is almost carried along like a cloud, like a dream, by the gentle breeze. . . . Blow a little harder, in longer breaths! . . . She rallies, drawing her arms closer to her bosom, which she covers more carefully, lest a puff of air become too bold, lest it insinuate itself, smooth and coolish, under the light covering . . . Her blush grows healthier, her cheeks become fuller, her eyes more limpid, her step firmer. Temptation tends to make a person more beautiful. Every young girl ought to fall in love with the zephyr, for no man is able thus to enhance her beauty while toying with her . . . Her body bends forward a little, she looks down toward the tips of her feet. . . .

Hold back a little! This is too much, her figure broadens, it loses its lovely slimness . . . Cool her a little! . . . It is refreshing, isn't it, dear girl, to feel these invigorating shivers after being warm? One is tempted to fling out one's arms in gratitude, in joy over existence . . . She half turns around . . . A strong gust now, so that I may divine the beauty of her form! A little stronger still, so that the folds of her dress cling more tightly to her body! . . . It is too much now! Her posture becomes unattractive, her light step encounters interference . . . Again she turns . . . Go ahead and blow now! Let her try her strength! . . . Enough, you go too far! One of her curls has become loosened . . . Will you restrain yourselves!

Behold, an entire regiment comes marching up:

The one is very much in love,
The other girl would like to be it.

Yes, it is undeniably a very unsatisfactory situation in life to
be walking abroad while leaning on the left arm of one's
future brother-in-law. This is about the same for a young girl
as being an assistant clerk is for a man. To be sure, the assistant clerk may be promoted, he has his place in the office and
is present on extraordinary occasions, which is not the sister-
in-law's lot; on the other hand, however, her advancement is
not so slow—if she is advanced and transferred to another
office . . . Blow a little more strongly now! When one has a
fixed point to hold on to, it is easier to offer resistance . . .
The center pushes forward vigorously, the wings cannot keep
up with it . . . He stands firm enough, the winds cannot budge
him, he is too heavy—but also too heavy for the wings to lift
him from the earth. He rushes forward in order to show—
that he is a heavy body; but the more unmoved he stands, the
more do the girls suffer because of it . . . Lovely ladies, may I
offer you a piece of good advice? Leave the future husband
and brother-in-law out of it, try to walk alone, you will find
that you will derive much more pleasure from doing so . . .
Blow more gently now! . . . How they are tossed about by the
wind's billows! Soon they will be moving down the street,
facing each other in the intricate evolutions of a dance—could
any dance music call forth a greater gayety? And yet the wind
does not tire out, it invigorates . . . Now they sweep along side
by side down the street, in full sail—could any waltz carry a
young girl along more seductively? And yet the wind does not
tire out, it supports . . . Now they turn around and face the
husband and brother-in-law . . . A little opposition is agreeable, is it not? One enjoys struggling for possession of what
one loves, and one will not fail to win what one is struggling
for. There is a Providence which comes to the aid of love; that
is why you see that the man has the wind in his favor . . .

Have I not arranged it well? When one has the wind at one's back, one can easily steer past the beloved, but when it blows against one, then one gets pleasantly agitated, one rushes to the beloved, and the gust of wind makes one sounder and more tempting and more alluring, and it cools the fruit of one's lips, which should be enjoyed cold, because it is so hot, just as champagne heats when it almost freezes . . . How they laugh and chatter! The wind carries their words away—what, after all, is there to talk about here? And again they laugh and bend before the wind and hold on to their hats and watch their feet . . . Stop now, lest the young girls become impatient or angry at us or afraid of us!—Just so, resolutely and forcefully, the right foot before the left. . . .

How boldly and challengingly she looks about in the world . . . Do I see right? She walks arm in arm with a man, therefore she must be engaged. Let me see, my child, what sort of a present you have received on life's Christmas tree . . . Ah yes, he appears to be a very reliable fiancé. She is, then, in the first stage of the engagement, she loves him—possibly so, and yet her love, wide and capacious, flutters loosely about him; she still owns the cloak of love, which can hide many . . . Blow up a little! . . . Yes, when one walks so rapidly, it is no wonder that the ribbons on one's hat tauten in the wind, so that they seem to be wings bearing along this light creature —and her love, which is like an elfin veil the wind plays with. Yes, when love is looked at in this manner, it seems so capacious; but when one is about to put it on, when the veil is to be altered to an everyday dress, then there is not enough material left for many ruches . . . God forbid! When one has had the courage to take a decisive step for one's entire life, one surely dares to walk straight against the wind. Who doubts it? Not I; but no temper, little lady, no temper! Time is a hard taskmaster, and the wind isn't bad either . . . Tease her a bit! . . . What became of the handkerchief? . . . Ah, you managed to recover it . . . One of the hatbands got loose . . . this is really most embarrassing for the fiancé, who is present . . .

There comes a girl friend whom you must greet. This is the first time she has seen you since you became engaged; after all, it is for the sake of showing yourself as an engaged girl that you are here on Bredgade and intend to continue your walk on Langelinie. As far as I know, it is customary for a newly wed couple to go to church the first Sunday after the wedding; an engaged couple, on the other hand, takes a stroll on Langelinie. Yes, generally speaking, it cannot be denied that an engagement has a great deal in common with Langelinie . . . Pay heed now, the wind seizes your hat, hold on to it, bend your head down . . . It is really most annoying that you didn't manage to greet your friend, that you lacked the calm necessary to greet with that superior air an engaged girl ought to assume toward an unengaged one . . . Blow a little more gently now! . . . The good days have arrived . . . How she clings to the beloved! She is so far ahead of him that she can turn her head back and look up at him and rejoice in him, her wealth, her good fortune, her hope, her future . . . Oh, my girl, you make too much of him. . . . Or does he not owe it to me and the wind that he looks so vigorous? And do you yourself not owe it to me and to the gentle breezes, which are healing you and helping you to forget your pain, that you look so bursting with vitality, so full of longing and expectation?

> And I won't have a student grim
> Who reads all night and frowns.
> No, I will have an officer trim
> Whose hat a feather crowns.

That is apparent at once, dear girl, there is something in your look . . . No, you are by no means served with a student . . . But why must it be an officer? Would a candidate, one who has completed his studies, not serve just as well? . . . At this moment, however, I cannot offer you either an officer or a candidate. Instead, I can serve you with cool tempering breezes . . .

Now blow up a bit! . . . That's right, throw the silk shawl back
over your shoulder, walk very slowly, then your cheek will
grow a little paler and the glow of your eyes less intense . . .
Yes, a little exercise, especially in such fine weather as we are
having today, plus a little patience, and you are bound to get
your officer.

Here come two who are meant for each other. What
firmness in their step, what confidence in their entire bearing,
based on mutual trust, what *harmonia praestabilita* in all their
movements, what self-satisfied thoroughness! Their attitudes
are not light and graceful, they do not dance with each other,
no, but there is a permanence in them, a bluffness that
awakens a hope that cannot be deceived, that inspires mutual
respect. I wager that their view of life is this: life is a way.
And to walk arm in arm together through life's joys and sorrows seems to be their destiny. They harmonize to such a degree that the lady does not even claim the privilege of walking
on the sidewalk. . . . But why do you fuss so about the couple?
They hardly seem to merit so much attention. Would there be
anything special to take note of? . . . But it is half past one, I
must be off to Høibroplads.

One would not believe it possible to calculate the history of
a soul's development with such fair accuracy. It shows how
sound Cordelia is. Verily, she is a remarkable girl. She is quiet,
modest, and undemanding, but unconsciously there is in her a
prodigious demand. I became aware of this today when I saw
her come in from outside. The slight resistance a gust of wind
can offer awakens, as it were, all the powers within her, without, however, calling forth an internal conflict. She is not an
insignificant little girl who vanishes between one's fingers, so
fragile that one almost fears she will go to pieces if one merely
looks at her; but neither is she a showy exhibition flower. Like
a physician I can therefore derive pleasure from observing all
the symptoms in this case history.

Gradually I am beginning to move closer to her in my attack, to go over to a more direct assault. If I were to indicate this change on my military map of the family, I should say, "I have moved my chair in such a way that I now sit with my side toward her." I take up with her more than before, I address her, I elicit answers from her. Her soul has passion and intensity, and without striving to be different by way of foolish and vain reflections, it has a craving for the uncommon. My irony over the ignobleness of human beings, my derision of their cowardice and their tepid indolence fascinate her. She obviously enjoys guiding the chariot of the sun across the arch of heaven, coming too close to the earth, and singeing people a little. However, she does not trust me; hitherto I have discouraged every rapprochement, even on the intellectual level. She must strengthen herself in herself before I let her lean on me. Momentarily it may indeed look as if it were she whom I would make my confidante in my freemasonry, but only momentarily. She must develop herself in herself, she must feel her soul's elasticity, she must try the weight of the world. What progress she is making, her rejoinders and her eyes easily show me; just once have I seen a devastating wrath in them. To me she must owe nothing, for she must be free; only in freedom is there love, only in freedom are there diversion and eternal pleasure. Even though I strive to have her fall into my arms with a nature-given inevitability, even though I strive to have her gravitate toward me, yet at the same time it is of the utmost importance that she does not fall like a heavy body but rather as spirit gravitates toward spirit. Even though she is to belong to me, this must not be in the unaesthetic sense of her resting upon me like a burden. She must neither be an incumbrance in the physical sense nor an obligation in a moral sense. Between us two there shall prevail only freedom's own play. I must find her so light that I can take her on my arm.

Cordelia occupies me almost too much. I again lose my balance, not in her presence, not when she is present, but when in the strictest sense I am alone with her. I long for her, not in order to talk with her, but only to let her image float past me; I steal after her when I know that she has gone out, not to be seen, but to see her. The other evening we left the Baxter residence together; Edvard accompanied her. In greatest haste I parted from them, turning quickly into another street, where my servant was waiting for me. In a jiffy I rechanged my clothes, and then met her again without her being aware of it. Edvard was as silent as always. In love I certainly am, but not in the ordinary sense, and in that respect one must be very cautious, since there always are dangerous consequences; and one is that way just once. Still the god of love is blind; if one is shrewd, one can easily fool him. The trick, as regards impressions, is to be as sensitive as possible, to know what impression one makes on each girl and what impression she makes on one. In this manner one can even be in love with many at the same time, because one is differently in love with each girl. To love just one is too little; to love all is to be superficial. To know one's self and to love as many as possible, to let one's soul conceal all the powers of love in itself in such a way that each girl gets her particular sustenance, while the consciousness embraces the whole—that is enjoyment, that means to live.

Edvard cannot really complain about me. To be sure, I want Cordelia to fall in love with him, I want her to get a distaste for ordinary love through him and consequently to transcend her own limitations, but for this very reason it is essential that Edvard should not be a caricature. Otherwise my plan would be futile. Not only is Edvard a good match in the bourgeois sense of the word (which is of no importance in her eyes, since to a seventeen-year-old girl such things are irrelevant), he himself has a number of attractive qualities which I try to help him show off in the most favorable light. Like a gentleman of the wardrobe I fit him out as well as the resources of the house allow; yes, sometimes I even adorn him with a little borrowed finery. When we thereupon betake ourselves to Cordelia's, I feel quite odd, walking at his side. It is as if he were my brother, my son, and yet he is my friend, of my age, and my rival. He can never become dangerous to me. Since he is destined to fall, the higher I manage to raise him, the better, the more conscious Cordelia becomes of what she scorns, the more intensely she senses what she desires. I make things easier for him, I commend him, in short, I do everything a friend can do for a friend. In order to emphasize my coldness, I sometimes even decry Edvard as an enthusiast. Since Edvard does not know how to help himself, I must project his image.

Cordelia hates and fears me. What does a young girl fear? Intellect. Why? Because intellect constitutes the negation of her entire feminine existence. Masculine beauty, a pleasant personality, and so forth, are good means. One can make a conquest with their aid, but without ever achieving a complete victory. Why? Because one is waging war upon a girl on her own terms, and where these prevail she is always the stronger. With the aid of those means, one can get a girl to blush, to cast down her eyes, but one can never call forth the indescribable, entrancing anxiety that makes her beauty interesting.

Non formosus erat, sed erat facundus Ulixes,
*et tamen aequoreas torsit amore Deas.**

Everyone ought to know his own abilities. But something that has often upset me is that even those who have natural talents conduct themselves in such a bungling manner. One really ought to be able to see at a glance in any young girl who has become the victim of another's love, or rather of her own love, just how she has been deceived. The practiced murderer employs a definite thrust, and experienced police are able to identify the perpetrator as soon as they have examined the wound. But where does one meet such systematic seducers, where such psychologists? The seduction of a girl means to most men the seduction of a girl, and that's that, and yet a whole language is concealed in this thought.

As a woman, she hates me; as a talented woman, she fears me; as one with a good mind, she loves me. This conflict I have called forth in her soul as a beginning. My pride, my defiance, my cold derision, my heartless irony, these tempt her, not as if she might wish to love me; no, surely there is no trace of such feelings in her, least of all toward me. She wants to vie with me. My proud independence of people, a freedom like that of the Arabs in the desert, is what attracts her. My laughter and singularity neutralize every erotic reaction. She is

---

* Ulysses was not handsome, but he was eloquent,/and therefore he caused the goddesses of the sea to be tormented with love for him. (Ovid, *Ars amandi*)

fairly free in her manner toward me, and in so far as there is
any reticence, it is more intellectual than feminine. She is so
far from regarding me as a lover that our relation to each
other is that of two good minds. She takes my hand, presses
it, laughs, and pays me a certain attention in a purely Greek
sense. Then when the ironist and the mocker have fooled her
long enough, I shall follow the suggestion found in the old
lay: "The knight spreads out his cape so red and bids the
maiden fair to sit on it." However, I do not spread out my
cape in order to sit with her on the greensward, but in order
to disappear with her into the air in the flight of thought. Or,
instead of taking her with me, I straddle a thought, wave farewell to her, blow her a kiss, and vanish from sight, audible
only in the soughing of the winged words; but unlike Jehovah
I do not become more manifest through the voice, rather less
and less so, for while I speak, I rise. Then she is eager to join
me in this bold flight of thought. But this lasts only a single
instant, the very next moment I am cold and pedantic.

There are different kinds of feminine blushes. There is the
coarse brick-red blush. Novelists have an abundant supply
of it, for they let their heroines blush all over. There is the delicate blush; it is the red of the spirit's dawn. In a young girl
it is priceless. The fleeting blush that accompanies a happy
idea is beautiful in a man, more beautiful in a youth, charming
in a woman. It is a flash of lightning, a heat lightning of the
spirit. It is most beautiful in a youth, charming in a girl, because it reveals its virginal quality and therefore also has the
modesty of surprise. The older one becomes, the more this
blush disappears.

At times I read aloud to Cordelia, generally things of no
particular interest. Edvard must as usual hold the candle, for
I have pointed out to him that a very good way to get into a
young girl's graces is to lend her books. He has indeed profited
by following my advice, for this puts her under obligation to
him. The chief gainer, however, am I, because I determine the

choice of books and yet remain an outsider. This enables me
to make my observations undisturbed. I can give Edvard
whatever books I wish, since he knows nothing about literature, I can venture whatever I wish, go to any extreme.
When we meet at Cordelia's in the evening, I pick up the
book in a seemingly casual manner, turn a few pages in it, read
half aloud, and praise Edvard for his attentiveness.

Last night I wished to test the elasticity of her spirit by an
experiment. I was undecided whether to have Edvard lend
her Schiller's *Poems,* so that I might accidentally come upon
Thekla's song, which I would then read aloud, or Bürger's
Poems. I chose the latter, particularly because his "Lenore"
is somewhat highflown, however beautiful the ballad is otherwise. I opened the volume at "Lenore" and read the poem
aloud with all the pathos I was capable of. Cordelia was moved,
she sewed with nervous haste, as if she were the one Wilhelm
had come to fetch. I paused. The aunt had listened without
emotional involvement; she fears no Wilhelms, whether dead
or alive; besides, her knowledge of German is limited. She was
quite in her element, however, when I showed her the beautifully bound copy and began a conversation about the art of
bookbinding. My purpose was to destroy in Cordelia the impression of the pathetic in the very moment in which it had
been awakened. She became somewhat anxious, but this anxiety, it was clear to me, did not entice her, it gave her an un-
canny feeling instead.

the 14th.

Today my eyes rested upon her for the first time. They say that sleep can make the eyelids so heavy that they close of themselves; perhaps this glance can produce a similar effect. Her eyes close, and yet dark forces stir within her. She does not see that I am looking at her, but she feels it, she feels it all over her body. Her eyes close, and it is night, but within her it is bright day.

Edvard must go. He is about to take the final step: at any moment I may expect him to go to her and make a declaration of love. There is no one who knows this better than myself, who am his confidant and who deliberately keep him in this state of exaltation, so that he can have a greater effect upon Cordelia. But to allow him to confess his love is too risky. I know very well that he will receive a refusal, but that will not be the end of the affair. He will certainly take it very much to heart, and this will perhaps move and touch Cordelia. Even though in such a case I do not need to fear the worst, namely, that she might reverse herself, still her soul's pride will possibly suffer injury through this pure sympathy. If this happens, then my whole plan concerning Edvard has failed completely.

My relation to Cordelia is slowly becoming dramatic. Something must happen, whatever it may be; if I remain a mere observer, I shall let the moment slip by. She must be taken by surprise, that is necessary; but if one wants to surprise her, one must be on the alert. Tactics that are surprising in general might not have the expected effect on her. She must really be surprised in such a way that in the first moment the reason for her surprise nearly is that something quite ordinary is happening. Gradually it must then appear that a surprising element was implicit in it, after all. This is also always the law for the interesting, and the interesting in turn is the law for all my movements with regard to Cordelia. If one knows how to surprise, the game is always won; for an instant one suspends the energy of the person concerned, one makes it impossible for her to act, and this happens whether one employs the ordinary or the extraordinary as means.

I still remember with a certain self-satisfaction a foolhardy experiment upon a lady of rank. In vain I had for some time been hanging around her in the hope of developing an interesting contact, but then one day I ran into her on the street. I was certain that she did not know who I was or that I resided here in town. She was walking alone. I stole past her in order to be able to meet her face to face. I stepped aside, she kept to the sidewalk. At this moment I cast a melancholy glance at her, I almost had tears in my eyes. I doffed my hat. She stopped. In a trembling voice and with a dreamy look I said, "Do not be angry, gracious lady, there is such a striking resemblance between your features and those of a person whom I love with all my soul, but who lives far away from me, that I am sure you will forgive me my strange conduct." She believed me to be a sentimentalist, and a young girl likes a bit of sentimentality, particularly when she feels superior and dares to smile about one. Yes, she smiled, and this smile was indescribably becoming to her. With dignified condescension she bowed to me and smiled. She moved on, I walked as much as two steps by her side. A few days later I met her, I took the liberty of greeting. She laughed at me . . . Patience is indeed a precious virtue, and he who laughs last, laughs best.

It would be possible to think of several means by which to surprise Cordelia. I might try to raise an erotic storm powerful enough to deracinate trees. With its help I might try, if possible, to sweep her off the ground, to tear her out of the historic continuity; to attempt in this agitation to arouse her passion by means of clandestine meetings. It is not inconceivable that this could be done. A man could induce a girl with her passion to do whatever he desired. However, it would be aesthetically wrong. I am not fond of vertigo, and this state is to be recommended only when one has to do with girls who can gain poetic glamor in no other way. Besides, one easily misses the real enjoyment, for too much confusion also is harmful. With her it would completely lose its effect. In a few draughts I would imbibe what might have refreshed me a long time, yes, what with peace of mind I might have enjoyed more fully and richly. Cordelia is not to be enjoyed in a state of exaltation. She might be surprised at first if I behaved in this manner, but she would soon be surfeited, precisely because this surprise lay too close to her bold soul.

Surely the best, the most expedient method of all is a pure and simple engagement. She will perhaps believe her ears even less if she hears me make a prosaic declaration of love, *item* ask for her hand, even less than if she listened to my impassioned eloquence, sipped my poisonous potion, heard her heart throb at the thought of an elopement.

The curse of an engagement is always the ethical element in it. The ethical is equally tiresome in learning as in life. What a difference! Under the heaven of the aesthetic everything is light, beautiful, ephemeral, but when the ethical appears on the scene, everything becomes hard, angular, infinitely boring. In a stricter sense, however, an engagement does not have ethical reality, as marriage does; it has validity only *ex consensu gentium.* This ambiguity can prove very useful to me. The ethical in it is just enough to give Cordelia eventually the impression that she is going beyond the bounds of the ordinary; at the same time the ethical in it is not so serious that I need fear a more critical upheaval. I have always had a certain respect for the ethical. Never have I given a girl a promise of marriage, not even a careless one; in so far as it might seem that I am doing it here, I say that it is only a feigned move. I shall certainly manage things in such a way that she will be the one who cancels the commitment. My pride disdains to give promises. I despise a judge who lures a sinner into confession by promising him liberty. Such a judge waives his power and ability.

Another circumstance affecting my *modus operandi* is that I desire nothing which is not, in the strictest sense, freedom's gift. Let crude seducers employ such methods. What, after all, do they achieve? Whoever is unable to captivate a girl to such an extent that she loses sight of everything he does not wish her to see, whoever is unable to pervade a girl's being to such an extent that it is from her that everything emanates as he wishes it, he is and remains a bungler; I do not envy him his enjoyment. Such a person is and remains a bungler, a seducer, something I certainly cannot be called. I am an aesthete, an eroticist, who has understood the nature of love and its *pointe,* who believes in love and knows it from the ground up, and the only reservation I make is the private opinion that every love affair lasts half a year at the most and that every relationship is over as soon as the ultimate has been enjoyed. All this I know, but I also know that to be loved, to be loved more than anything else in the world, is the highest enjoyment imaginable. To pervade a girl's being is an art, to recede from it is a masterpiece. Still, the latter depends essentially on the former.

There is still another method possible. I could arrange everything so as to get her engaged to Edvard. I would then become the friend of the family. Edvard would trust me unconditionally, for, after all, he would owe his happiness to me. In this way I would gain the advantage of being better concealed. But no, that is no good. She cannot become engaged to Edvard without losing in stature. An additional factor would be that my relationship to her would then become more piquant than interesting. The infinite prosaism inherent in an engagement is precisely the sounding board of the interesting.

Everything is becoming more significant in the Wahl household. One distinctly notes that a hidden life is stirring beneath the daily routine and that this life must soon proclaim itself in a corresponding revelation. The Wahl household is preparing for an engagement. A superficial observer might imagine that the aunt and I were about to become a pair. What might not be achieved by such a union for the dissemination of agricultural knowledge in the following generation! Thus I would then become Cordelia's uncle. I am a friend of the freedom of thought, and no thought is so absurd that I lack the courage to entertain it. Cordelia fears a declaration of love from Edvard, Edvard hopes that such a declaration will decide everything. And of that he may be sure. However, in order to spare him the awkward consequences of such a step, I shall try to forestall him. I hope soon to be able to give him his discharge papers, he is very much in the way now. I was greatly aware of that today. Does he not look so dreamy and intoxicated with love that one almost fears he will suddenly arise like a somnambulist and in the presence of the whole assembly confess his love with such objective vividness that it will not seem to concern Cordelia? I gave him a sharp look today. Just as an elephant seizes an object with its trunk, so I picked up Edvard, all of him, with my eyes and tossed him backward. Although he remained seated, I do believe that he had a corresponding sensation all over his body.

Cordelia is not so assured in her demeanor toward me as formerly. She used to approach me with a womanly assurance, but now she wavers a little. This is hardly very significant, however, and I should not find it difficult to bring back everything to the old footing. But that I refuse to do. Just one more exploration, and then the engagement. There can be no difficulties in this regard. Cordelia, surprised, says yes, the aunt utters a hearty amen. She will be beside herself with joy over such an agricultural son-in-law. Son-in-law! How everything hangs together like burs when one ventures into this territory. I do not really become her son-in-law, but only her nephew, or rather, *volente deo,* neither.

Today I reaped the fruit of a rumor which I had caused to circulate, that I was in love with a young girl. With Edvard's help it also reached Cordelia's ears. She is curious, she watches me, but she does not dare to ask questions, and yet it is not unimportant to her to gain certainty, partly because it seems incredible to her, partly because she would be tempted to see in this a precedent for herself; for if such a cold scoffer as myself can fall in love, then she could do the same without needing to feel ashamed.

Today I brought up the matter. I believe that I am able to tell a story so that the point is not lost, *item,* so that it isn't given away too soon. To keep those who listen to my story *in suspenso,* to ascertain by means of diversions of an episodic nature what they wish its outcome to be, to fool them in the course of the narration, that is my pleasure; to employ amphibolies, so that the listeners give one meaning to what has been said and then suddenly notice that the words can also be interpreted differently, that is my art. If one desires a good opportunity to make certain observations, one should always deliver a speech. In conversation the person concerned finds it easier to be elusive, by means of questions and answers he can better conceal the impression one's words produce.

With solemn seriousness I began my speech to the aunt: "Am I to impute the rumor to the benevolence of my friends or to the malice of my enemies, and who does not have too much of the one and the other?" Here the aunt made a comment which I helped to elaborate with all my might, so as to keep Cordelia, who was listening, in suspense, a suspense she could not shake off, since it was her aunt I was talking with and my mood was solemn. I continued: "Or shall I attribute it to an accident, to the *generatio aequivoca* of a rumor (this expression Cordelia obviously did not understand, it only confused her, all the more as I uttered it with false emphasis and with a sly mien, as if the point lay here) that I, who am wont to live in seclusion from the world, have become the object of gossip to the effect that I am engaged?" As it was quite apparent that Cordelia was still anxious to hear my explanation, I continued: "To my friends, since it must be regarded as good fortune to fall in love (Cordelia made a startled movement in one direction), to my enemies, since it must be regarded as particularly absurd if this happiness should fall to my lot (movement in the opposite direction), or to accident, since there is not the slightest foundation for it, or to the rumor's *generatio aequivoca,* since the whole business may well have originated in a hollow head's thoughtless intercourse with itself?" The aunt was dying with feminine curiosity to learn the identity of the lady with whom one had been pleased to associate me, but every query in this direction was waved aside. On Cordelia the whole story made a strong impression, I almost believe that Edvard's stock rose a few points.

The decisive moment is drawing near. I might address myself to the aunt with a written request for Cordelia's hand. This is indeed the usual procedure in affairs of the heart, as if it were more natural for the heart to write than to speak. What might induce me to choose this procedure is precisely its philistine quality, but if I choose it, then I lose the essential element of surprise, and that I cannot forego.

If I had a friend, he would perhaps say to me, "Have you considered well this very serious step you are taking, a step which is decisive for all the rest of your life and for another being's happiness?" Receiving such advice is an advantage that

comes from having a friend. Well, I have no friend; whether
this is an advantage, I shall leave undecided, but I regard
being free from his advice an absolute advantage. For the rest,
I have thoroughly pondered the whole matter in the strictest
sense of the word.

On my side there is nothing now to prevent the engagement. I therefore go a-courting. Who would surmise such a
thing from looking at me? Soon my humble person will be regarded from a higher standpoint. I stop being a person and
become—a match; yes, a good match, the aunt will say. The
one I feel most sorry for is the aunt, for she loves me with such
a pure and sincere agricultural love, she almost adores me as
her ideal.

To be sure, in the course of my life I have made many dec-
larations of love, and yet all my experience avails me not
in the least here; for this declaration must be made in a very
special way. What I must principally impress upon my mind
is that the whole business is nothing but a feint. I have con-
ducted several rehearsals in order to determine which course
would be the best one for me to take. To make the moment
erotic would be risky, since that might easily anticipate what
is to come later and be unfolded gradually. To make it very
serious is dangerous; such a moment is so significant for a
young girl that her soul can become as fixed in it as a dying
man's in his last will. To make it hearty, farcical, would harmonize neither with the mask I have hitherto used nor with
the one I intend to put on and wear. To make it witty and
ironic is to be too daring. If all I wanted was to elicit a little
yes, as is generally the case with people in this situation, then
it would be as easy as adding two and two. This is indeed
important to me, but it is not of supreme importance; for
although I have chosen this girl, although I have centered
much attention, indeed all my interest, upon her, yet there are
certain conditions under which I would not accept her yes. I
am not at all intent upon possessing the girl in the external

sense, what I want to do is to enjoy her in the artistic sense. Therefore my beginning must be as artistic as possible. The beginning must be as unresolved as possible, it must be omnipotential. If she immediately regards me as a deceiver, then she misunderstands me, for in the ordinary sense I am not a deceiver; if she regards me as a faithful lover, then she also misunderstands me. What is essential is that this scene should determine her soul as little as possible. At such a moment a girl's soul is as prophetic as a dying person's. This must be prevented.

My charming Cordelia! I cheat you out of something beautiful, but it cannot be otherwise, and I shall compensate you as well as I can. The whole scene must be kept as insignificant as possible, so that she will be unable, after she has given me her yes, to throw the least light upon what may be concealed in this relationship. This infinite possibility is precisely the interesting. If she is able to predict anything, then I have proceeded wrongly and the whole relationship loses its meaning. That she might say yes because she loves me is unthinkable, for she does not love me at all. It would be best if I could transform the engagement from an act to an incident, from something she does to something that happens to her, about which she must say, "God only knows how it actually happened."

the 31st.

Today I have written a love letter for a third party. This is something I always enjoy doing. In the first place, it is always quite interesting to enter into such a situation and yet lose none of one's comfort. I fill my pipe, I listen to the account, and the letters from the intended are submitted to me. The way a young girl writes is always a source of important studies for me. There he sits, in love like a mooncalf, and reads her letters to me—occasionally I interrupt him with a laconic comment: she writes well, she has feeling, good taste, she is cautious, no doubt she has been in love before, and so on. In the second place, I am doing a good deed. I am helping to bring two young people together, and then I strike a balance. For every happy couple I select a victim for myself; I make two people happy, at the most I render only one person unhappy. I am scrupulous and trustworthy. I have never deceived anyone who has entrusted himself to me. There is a bit of fun at other people's expense involved, but this, after all, is a lawful perquisite. And why do I enjoy this trust? Because I know Latin and pursue my studies and because I always keep my little affairs to myself. And do I not deserve this trust? I certainly never misuse it.

August 2nd.

The moment had arrived. I caught a glimpse of the aunt on the street and therefore knew that she would not be at home. Edvard was at the customhouse. Consequently it was likely that Cordelia would be alone. And so she was. She was sitting at the sewing table, occupied with some needlework. I have visited the family very rarely in the forenoon, and so she became slightly perturbed upon seeing me. The situation was close to becoming emotional. Had this happened, the fault would not have been hers, for she regained her composure rather easily; I was the one who felt moved, for despite my reserve she made an unusually strong impression upon me. How charming she was in her simple, blue-striped calico house dress, with a freshly plucked rose at her bosom—a freshly plucked rose, nay, the girl herself was like a freshly plucked rose, so fresh, so untouched. Who, after all, knows where a young girl passes the night? In the land of illusions, I imagine, but each morning she returns from there, and this explains her youthful freshness. She looked so young and yet so ready for life, as if Nature, like a tender and bountiful mother, had released her from her care only then. I seemed to witness this farewell scene. I saw how the loving mother once again embraced her in farewell and I heard her say, "Go out into the world, my child, I have done everything for you. Take this kiss as a seal upon your lips, it is a seal which guards the sanctuary. No one can break it, unless you yourself will it, but when the right one comes, you will understand him." And she pressed a kiss upon her lips, a kiss unlike a human kiss, which takes something, no, a divine kiss, which gives everything, which gives the girl the power of the kiss.

Marvelous Nature, how profound and mysterious you are! You give to the man the word and to the girl the eloquence of the kiss! This kiss was on her lips, and the farewell on her brow, and the glad greeting in her eyes; therefore she looked at the same time so much at home, for she was indeed the child of the house, and so much a stranger, for she did not know the world, but only the tender mother, who watched invisibly over her. She was indeed charming and childlike, and yet adorned with a noble virginal dignity that inspired reverence.

But soon I was again unemotional and solemnly stolid, as is proper when one would do something significant in a manner that renders it insignificant. After a few general remarks I moved a bit nearer to her and voiced my request. A human being who talks like a book is extremely tiresome to listen to; at times, however, it is quite appropriate to speak in that way, for a book has the remarkable quality that it can be interpreted at will. One's speech also acquires this quality when one talks like a book. I limited myself in a very sober manner to the customary phrases. It cannot be denied that she was as surprised as I had expected her to be. To describe just how she looked is difficult. Her expressions were manifold, rather like the promised, but still unpublished, commentary to my book, a commentary that will lend itself to every possible interpretation. One word, and she would have laughed at me; one word, and she would have been moved; one word, and she would have avoided me; but no word crossed my lips. I remained stolidly serious and stuck to the ritual.—"She had known me but a short time." Good God, such difficulties one encounters only on the narrow path of an engagement, never on the primrose path of love.

Strange indeed! When during the preceding days I considered the matter, I did not hesitate to assume that, taken by surprise, she would say yes. There you see what all such preparations avail. This was not the outcome, for she said neither yes nor no, but referred me to her aunt. I should have foreseen this. Luck, however, was really with me, for this denouement was even better.

The aunt gives her consent; I never harbored the slightest doubt in that respect. Cordelia accepts her advice. As for my engagement, I do not boast that it is poetic; on the contrary, it is in every way philistine and commonplace. The girl doesn't know whether to say yes or no; the aunt says yes, the girl also says yes; I take the girl, she takes me—and now the story begins.

And so I am engaged, Cordelia also is engaged, and that is about all she knows concerning the matter. If she had a girl friend with whom she might talk freely, she would perhaps say, "I don't really understand what it all means. There is something about him that attracts me, but what it is I cannot figure out. He has a strange power over me, but love him I do not and perhaps never shall. On the other hand, I shall most likely be able to endure living with him and may therefore become quite happy with him, for he will surely not demand a great deal if only one stays with him." My dear Cordelia, perhaps he will demand a great deal more and in exchange for that ask for less staying power!

Of all ridiculous things an engagement surely is the most ridiculous. Marriage, after all, has a meaning, even if I may find this meaning bothersome. An engagement is a purely human invention and by no means does credit to its inventor. It is neither one thing nor another and bears the same relation to love as the frill hanging down the beadle's back to the professor's gown.

So now I am a member of this honorable company. This is not without significance for it is true, as Trop says, that only by first being an artist oneself does one acquire the right to judge other artists. And is not a fiancé also a circus artist?

Edvard is beside himself with bitterness. He lets his beard grow, he has put away his black frock coat, which is very indicative. He wants to talk with Cordelia, wants to describe my

DIARY OF A SEDUCER

underhandedness to her. It will be a touching scene: Edvard
unshaven, carelessly dressed, talking at the top of his voice to
Cordelia. If only he does not cut me out with his long beard!
Vainly I try to bring him to reason, I explain that it is the aunt
who has brought about the match, that Cordelia perhaps still
harbors tender feelings for him, that I shall be willing to bow
out if he can win her. For a moment he hesitates, asking himself whether he should not have his beard clipped in a new
way, buy a new black frock coat, but in the next instant he be-
rates me. I do everything I can to keep on good terms with
him. However angry he may be with me, I am certain that he
will take no step without consulting me; he does not forget the
benefits he has obtained from me as mentor. And why should
I deprive him of the last hope, why should I break with him?
He is a good man, and who knows what may happen in the
future?

What I have to do now is, on the one hand, to make all the
necessary preparations for getting the engagement voided, thus
assuring myself of a more beautiful and significant relation to
Cordelia, and on the other hand, to employ the time as well
as possible by taking delight in all the grace, all the loveliness,
with which nature has so abundantly endowed her, by taking
delight in them, but with the restraint and circumspection
that prevent any foretaste. When I have brought matters to
the point where she has learned what it means to love, and
what it means to love me, then the engagement will break like
an imperfect mold, and she will belong to me. Others become
engaged when they have reached this point, and they then
may look forward to a boring marriage for all eternity. But
that is their concern.

Everything is still *in statu quo,* but no fiancé can be happier,
no miser who has found a gold coin can be more exhilarated
than I am. The thought that she is in my power intoxicates
me. A pure, innocent feminity, transparent as the sea and
as profound, without presentiment of love! Now she is to

learn what a power love is. Like a princess who has been raised from the dust to the throne of her ancestors, so shall she now be installed in the kingdom where she belongs. And this is to happen through me, and as she learns to love, she learns to love me; as she develops the rule, the paradigm is gradually revealed, and this is myself. As through love she becomes aware of her full significance, she will devote it to loving me, and when she senses that she has learned this from me, she will love me twice as much. The thought of my joy so overwhelms me that I nearly lose my cool detachment.

Her soul has not become volatile or slack because of the vague stirrings of love, as is the case with many young girls who never really get to know love, that is to say, unequivocally, energetically, totally. They have in their consciousness a vague, nebulous image, which is supposed to be an ideal according to which the real is to be tested. From such nebulosities there emerges a something with which one may manage to get through the world in a Christian way.

Now as love awakens in her soul, I gaze through it, I listen to it as it emanates from her with all the voices of love. I ascertain how it has taken shape in her, and I fashion myself in its likeness. And just as I am already directly involved in the story which love unfolds in her heart, so I again approach her from the outside, as deceptively as possible. After all, a girl loves but once.

Now I am in lawful possession of Cordelia, I have her aunt's consent and blessing, the congratulations of friends and relatives; that ought to suffice. Now the hardships of war are over, now begin the blessings of peace. How stupid! As if the aunt's blessing and the congratulations of friends could put me in possession of Cordelia in the real sense, as if the contrast between wartime and peacetime existed in love, which on the contrary is uninterrupted combat as long as it lasts, even if the weapons are different. The difference really is whether it is fought *cominus* or *eminus*. The more a love affair has been waged *eminus,* the more regrettable, for the less significant becomes the hand-to-hand fighting. To the latter belong a hand clasp as well as contact with the foot, something which Ovid, as is well known, both warmly recommends and jealously rants against, to say nothing of a kiss, an embrace.

He who fights *eminus* must generally depend on his eye alone, and yet, if he is an artist, he will know how to use this weapon with such virtuosity that nearly the same results are achieved. He can let his eye rest upon a girl with a desultory tenderness which has the same effect as if he accidentally touched her; he will be able to grasp her as firmly with his eye as if he held her locked in his arms. It will always be a fault, however, or a misfortune, if one fights *eminus* too long, for such a combat must ever be only an intimation, never the enjoyment itself. Only when one fights *cominus,* does everything attain its true significance. When the element of combat is lacking in love, it has ceased to be. I have virtually never fought *eminus* and therefore I am now not at the end, but at the beginning; I am readying my weapons. To be sure, I am in possession of her, that is, in a juridical and bourgeois sense, but nothing at all follows from that as far as I am concerned; I have far purer ideas. She is engaged to me, that is true, but if from this I were to conclude that she loved me, it would be a deception, for she is not at all in love. I am in lawful possession of her, and yet I do not possess her, just as I can possess a girl without being in lawful possession of her.

> *Auf heimlich erröthender Wange*
> *Leuchtet des Herzens Glühen.**

She sits on the sofa by the tea table and I sit on a chair at her side. This position has an intimate quality and at the same time a detaching dignity. The position is always extremely important, that is, for the person who has an eye for it. Love

* On the secretly blushing cheek/is reflected the glow of the heart. (Source unknown)

has many positions, this is the first one. How regally nature has endowed this girl; her pure, soft forms, her limpid eyes, her deep feminine innocence—all these intoxicate me.

I called on her. She came toward me with a glad expression as usual, but at the same time in a somewhat embarrassed, diffident manner; the engagement cannot fail to alter our relationship somewhat, but she does not know just how. She shook hands with me, but without the usual smile. I returned the greeting with a slight, barely noticeable pressure of the hand; I was gentle and friendly, without, however, being erotic.

She sits on the sofa by the tea table and I sit on a chair at her side. A transfiguring solemnity suffuses the scene, a soft matutinal radiance. She is silent; nothing interrupts the stillness. Gently my eyes steal over her, without desire, which here would be impudent. A delicate, fleeting blush passes over her, like a cloud over a meadow, rising and descending. What does this blush mean? Is it love, is it yearning, hope, fear? For is not the heart's color red? By no means. She wonders, she is surprised—not at me, that would be offering her too little; she is surprised, not at herself, but within herself, she is transformed within herself. This moment demands stillness; therefore let no reflection disturb it, let not the excitement of passion interrupt it. It is as if I were not present, and yet it is precisely my presence that provides the condition for her contemplative wonder. My being is in harmony with hers. In such a state a young girl is worshiped and adored like certain deities by silence.

It is fortunate indeed that I have my uncle's house. If I wished to instill a distaste for tobacco in a young man, I should take him to one of the smoking rooms in the home for university students. If I desire to instill a distaste for being engaged in a young girl, I need only bring her to this place. As in the guildhall of the tailors only tailors foregather, so here only engaged couples get together. It is a frightful company to fall into, and I cannot blame Cordelia for becoming impatient.

When we are assembled *en masse,* we muster about ten couples besides the extra battalions which the chief festivals of the year bring to the capital. Then we engaged couples can fully enjoy the pleasures of being engaged. I visit this alarm post with Cordelia in order to instill in her a distaste for these maudlin commonplaces, these boorish antics of lovesick artisans. Incessantly, throughout the evening, one hears a sound as if someone were going about with a fly swatter—it is the sound of lovers exchanging kisses. The atmosphere in this house is delightfully *sans gêne;* no one retires to the dark corners. No, they all sit about a large round table. I pretend to treat Cordelia in the same way. To this end I must do violence to my own feelings. It would really be outrageous if I were to allow myself to offend her deep femininity in this manner. I would reproach myself more for doing so than for deceiving her. In general, I can assure every girl who cares to entrust herself to me of perfect aesthetic treatment; only it ends with her being deceived. But this is also a part of my aesthetic creed, for either the girl deceives the man or the man deceives the girl. It would certainly be interesting if some literary hack could be induced to count up in fairy tales, legends, folksongs, and mythologies who is more frequently faithless, the man or the girl.

By no means do I regret the time that Cordelia costs me, although she takes up a good deal. Every meeting demands long preparations. I experience with her the birth and growth of her love. I am almost invisibly present when I sit visibly beside her. My conduct toward her is as when a dance, which should really be danced by two, is danced by one person alone. I am the other dancer, the invisible one. She moves as in a dream, and yet she dances with another, and this other is myself, who am invisible in so far as I am visibly present and visible in so far as I am invisible. The movements of the dance require a partner; she bends in his direction, she gives him her hand, she flees, she draws near him again. I take her hand, I

complete her thought, which, however, has already completed
itself. She moves to her soul's own melody; I am only
the occasion for her movement. I am not erotic, that would
merely serve to awaken her; I am pliant, supple, impersonal,
almost like a mood.

What does an affianced couple usually talk about? To my
knowledge, the two busily acquaint each other with the boring facts of their respective families. No wonder, then, that
the erotic element disappears! If one does not know how to
make love the absolute, in comparison with which everything
else is unimportant, one should never become involved with
love, even if one gets married ten times. Whether I have an
aunt called Mariane, an uncle called Christopher, a father who
is a major, and so on and so forth, all such revelations are irrelevant to the mysteries of love. Yes, even one's own past is
nothing. A young girl usually does not have much of importance to tell in this respect; if she has, then it may be worth
the trouble to listen to her, but, as a rule, not to love her. I for
my part do not seek histories, I have plenty of those. What I
seek is immediacy. It is the eternal element in love that the individuals first come into being for one another in the moment
of love.

A little confidence must be awakened in her, or, rather, a
doubt must be removed. I do not really belong to the class of
lovers who love one another out of respect, get married out of
respect, get children out of respect, but still I know very well
that love, especially as long as passion has not been aroused,
demands that the person who is its object should not offend
aesthetically against the moral. In this respect love has its own
dialectic. Thus, while my relation to Edvard is far more repre-
hensible from the moral standpoint than my behavior toward
the aunt, I shall find it much easier to justify the former to
Cordelia than the latter. She has said nothing as yet, but I
have nevertheless considered it best to explain to her the necessity for my conduct. The caution I employed flatters her

pride, the secretiveness with which I managed everything captures her attention. To be sure, it may seem that I have here already betrayed too much erotic refinement, that I shall contradict myself when later I am obliged to imply that I have never been in love before. That, however, does not matter. I am not afraid to contradict myself as long as she does not notice it and I attain what I want. Let learned disputants take pride in avoiding every contradiction; a young girl's life is too abundant not to have contradiction in it and consequently to make contradiction necessary.

She is proud and at the same time has no real conception of the erotic. Whereas she now defers to me intellectually to a certain degree, yet it is quite possible that when the erotic begins to assert itself, she may decide to turn her pride against me. Everything I observe indicates that she has no clear conception of woman's real significance. Therefore it was easy to arouse her pride against Edvard. This pride, however, was wholly eccentric, because she had no conception of love. If she acquires this, then she also acquires her true pride, but a remainder of that eccentric pride might easily be added to it. It would be conceivable, then, that she might turn against me. Although she will not regret having given her consent to the engagement, still she will easily see that I got it at no great cost to myself; she will realize that the beginning on her part was not made properly. If this dawns upon her, she will dare to offer me opposition. Let it be thus. Then I shall find out for certain how deeply she is moved.

Just as I expected! Already from far down the street I see this pretty little curly head stretching as far as possible out of the window. This is the third day that I have noticed it . . . Surely a young girl does not stand at a window for nothing, no doubt she has her good reasons . . . But for heaven's sake, I beg you not to stretch so far out of the window; I wager you are standing on the rung of a chair, I infer that from your position. Think how terrible it would be if you lost your balance and fell, not on my head, for I am keeping out of this, at least for the time being, but on his head, on his, for of course a "he" is involved. . . . Well, what do I see? From the distance approaches my friend, Licentiate Hansen, walking down the middle of the street. There is something unusual in his appearance, he doesn't propel himself forward in the usual manner, his longing seems to lend wings to his feet. Can he be a regular visitor in this house, and I not know about it? . . .

My fair lady, you have disappeared. I imagine that you have gone to open the door for him . . . Just come back, he is not going to enter the house, after all. . . . What, you think you know better? Well, I can assure you he said so himself. If the vehicle that just drove past had not made such a racket, you could have heard him say so yourself. I asked him in a very *en passant* manner, "Are you going in here?" He replied unequivocally, "No."

Now you can really bid him farewell, for the licentiate and I are going to take a walk. He is embarrassed, and embarrassed people usually are loquacious. Now I shall talk with him about the benefice he is seeking . . . Farewell, my fair lady, now we shall betake ourselves to the customhouse. Then, when we are out there, I shall say to him, "Confound it, you have taken me out of my way. I wanted to go up Vestergade."

Now look, here we are again! . . . What constancy! She is still standing in the window. Such a girl ought to make a man happy . . . And why am I doing all this, you ask? Because I am a mean person who gets his fun by teasing others? Not at all. I do it out of concern for you, my charming lady. In the first place: you have waited for the licentiate, you have longed for him, and so when he comes, he is twice as attractive. In the second place: when the licentiate passes through the door, he will say, "We almost gave ourselves away that time! The bloody chap stood in the doorway just as I wanted to visit you.

But I was clever, I involved him in a long chat about the pre-
ferment I am trying to get. I drew him away from here and
walked him as far as the customhouse. I am positive that he
noticed nothing." And then what? Now you are even fonder
of the licentiate than before, for you have always believed that
he had an exceptional intellect, but that he is also clever . . .
well, now you see it yourself. And that you have me to thank
for.

But something else occurs to me. Their engagement cannot
yet have been announced, otherwise I should have heard of it.
The girl is beautiful and sweet to look at, but she is young.
Perhaps her insight has not yet matured. Is it not conceivable
that she is carelessly undertaking a very serious step? This
must be prevented; I must have a talk with her. I owe her that,
for she is certainly a very charming girl. I owe it to the licentiate, for he is my friend; therefore I owe it to her again, for
she is my friend's intended. I owe it to the family, for it is certainly a highly respectable one. I owe it to the whole human
race, for it is a good deed. The whole human race! A great
thought, an inspiring deed, to act in the name of the whole
human race, to possess such wide authority!

But now to Cordelia! I always have use for mood, and the
girl's beautiful longing has really moved me.

Now commences the first war with Cordelia, in which I flee
and thereby teach her to be victorious in pursuing me. I constantly retreat before her, and in this retreat I teach her to
know through me all the power of love, its restless thoughts, its
passion, what longing is, and hope, and impatient expectation.
As I act out all this before her, the corresponding power and
emotions are developed in her. It is a triumphal procession in
which I lead her, and I am equally the one who sings dithy-
rambs to her victory and the one who shows her the way. She
will gain courage to believe in love, to believe that it is an eter-

nal power, when she sees its dominion over me, when she sees my emotions. She will believe me, partly because I have confidence in my art, partly because truth forms the basis of what I am doing. If this were not the case, she would not believe me. With each movement I make, she grows stronger and stronger. Love awakens in her soul and she is initiated into her significance as a woman.

Hitherto I have not wooed her as this word is understood in middle-class circles. What I am doing now is to set her free, for only thus will I love her.* She must never suspect that she owes this freedom to me, for then she would lose her self-confidence. When she feels free, so free that she is almost tempted to break with me, then the second war begins. Now she has power and passion, now the war has significance for me, let the immediate consequences be what they may. Suppose she becomes giddy with pride, suppose she breaks with me; very well, she has her freedom, but to me she shall belong nevertheless. To expect that the engagement should bind her would be absurd; only in her freedom will I possess her. Let her forsake me, the second war will begin in any case, and in this second war I shall be the victor just as surely as she was the victor in the first one in appearance only. The greater the abundance of her strength, the more interesting it is for me. The first war is a war of liberation; it is a game. The second is a war of conquest; it is a life-and-death struggle.

Do I love Cordelia? Yes. Sincerely? Yes. Faithfully? Yes—in an aesthetic sense, and surely this also holds significant meaning. What would it avail this girl if she had fallen into the hands of a dolt of a faithful husband? What would have become of her? Nothing. It is said that it takes a little more than honesty to get through life; I should say that it takes a little more than honesty to love such a girl. That more I have —it is falseness. And yet I love her faithfully. Austerely and soberly I watch over myself, so that everything there is in her,

* The passage contains an untranslatable pun based on the verb *at fri til,* "to propose to," "woo," and the adjective *fri,* "free."

the whole divine, rich nature in her, may be unfolded. I am one of the few who can do this, she is one of the few who are fitted for this. Are we then not suited to each other?

———————

Is it sinful of me that instead of looking at the minister I fix my eyes on the beautiful embroidered handkerchief you are holding in your hand? Is it sinful of you to hold it thus? . . . There is a name in one corner. . . . Charlotte Hahn is your name? . . . It is entrancing to learn a lady's name in such a casual manner. It is as if there were a ministering spirit who mysteriously made me acquainted with you. . . . Or is it no accident that the handkerchief is folded in such a way that I get to see the name? . . . You are moved, you wipe a tear from your eye. . . . The handkerchief again hangs limply down. . . . You are aware that I am looking at you and not at the minister. You glance at your handkerchief, you notice that it has betrayed your name. . . . It really is a very harmless matter, it is so easy to find out a girl's name. . . . Why must you now take it out on the handkerchief, why must it be crumpled up? Why are you angry at it, why are you angry at me? Listen to what the parson is saying, "Let no one lead a human being into temptation; even the one who does so unwittingly bears a responsibility, even he is in debt to the other, a debt which he can discharge only by increased good will." . . . Now he says amen. Outside the church door you may let your handkerchief flutter freely in the wind . . . or have you become afraid of me? What have I done? . . . Have I done more than you can forgive, than you dare remember—in order to forgive?

———————

A double movement becomes necessary with regard to Cordelia. If I always merely fled before her superior might, it would be possible that the erotic in her became too dissolute

and diffuse to allow the deeper womanliness to hypostatize itself. Then, when the second war began, she would be unable
to offer resistance. To be sure, she attains to her victory while
sleeping, that is as it should be; but, on the other hand, she
must constantly be awakened. Then, when for an instant it
looks as if her victory were about to be torn from her, she
must learn to want to hold on to it. In this conflict her womanhood is matured.

I could employ either conversations to excite or letters to
calm, or vice versa. The latter method is preferable in every
way. I then enjoy her most ardent moments. When she has
received a letter, when its sweet poison has mingled with her
blood, then a word is enough to make her love break forth.
The very next moment irony and a frosty manner arouse doubt,
but not to such a degree that they prevent her from continuing
to feel conscious of victory, to feel even more conscious of it
upon receipt of the next letter. Irony, moreover, does not lend
itself well to use in letters, for one runs the risk of her not understanding it. Passionate feelings can be intimated only
briefly in a conversation. My personal presence prevents the
ecstatic mood. When I am present in a letter only, she can easily suffer me, she confuses me to a certain extent with a universal being who lives in her love. In a letter, too, I can cast
restraint to the winds, in a letter I can flamboyantly throw
myself at her feet, I can do all sorts of things that would be
perfectly absurd if done in her presence and that would completely destroy the illusion. The contradiction in these movements will call forth and develop, strengthen and consolidate
the love in her, in one word, tempt it.

These letters must not, however, assume a strongly erotic
coloring too soon. In the beginning it is best for them to have
a somewhat general character, to contain single suggestions,
remove single doubts. Occasionally they may also intimate the
advantage an engagement gives one in keeping people away
by means of mystifications. What imperfections it otherwise

possesses, she shall not lack opportunities to discover. In my uncle's house I have a caricature I can point to whenever necessary. The truly erotic she cannot develop without my help. When I refuse her this help and let this distorted image torture her, then she will soon become tired of being engaged, without, however, being able to say that I am the one who made her tired of it.

A short letter will today give her an inkling of the state of her inner life by describing the condition of my soul. This is the correct method, and method I never lack. I have you to thank for that, you dear maidens, whom I once loved. To you I owe it that my soul is so attuned that I can be for Cordelia whatever I wish. With gratitude I remember you, the honor belongs to you. I shall always acknowledge that a young girl is a born teacher, from whom one can always learn, if nothing else, then at least how to deceive her—for this one learns best from the girls themselves. No matter how old I may become, I shall never forget that a man is not really through until he has grown so old that he can learn nothing from a young girl.

My Cordelia!

You say that you had not imagined me to be like this, but neither had I imagined that I could become like this. Does the change lie in you? For it is conceivable that I am not really changed, but that the eye with which you behold me is changed. Or does the change lie in me? It lies in me, for I love you; it lies in you, for it is you I love. By the cold, calm light of reason I considered everything proudly and dispassionately; nothing alarmed me. Even had an apparition knocked at my door, I should fearlessly have taken the candelabrum and opened up. But lo, I opened the door not to apparitions, to pale, flaccid forms, I opened it to you, my Cordelia, to life and youth and health and beauty, who entered in. My arm trembles, I cannot hold the light steady, I retreat before you, and yet I cannot desist from fixing my eyes upon you, I cannot desist from wishing that I might hold the light steady. Changed I am, but what is the nature of this change, why and how does it exist? I do not know, I cannot supply a better definition, I cannot use a richer predicate than to say about myself in an infinitely mysterious manner: I am changed.

Your Johannes

My Cordelia!

Love loves secrecy—an engagement is a revelation. It loves silence—an engagement is a public announcement. It loves whispering—an engagement is a loud proclamation. And yet, with my Cordelia's artful help, an engagement becomes a splendid device for deceiving the enemies. On a dark night there is nothing more dangerous to other vessels than hanging out a lantern that is more deceptive than the darkness.

Your Johannes

She sits on the sofa by the tea table and I sit at her side. She has her arm under mine; her head, weighed down by many thoughts, rests on my shoulder. She is so close to me and yet so far away; she surrenders herself to me and yet she does not belong to me. There is still resistance on her part, but this resistance is not subjectively reflective, it is the ordinary feminine resistance, for woman's nature is surrender in the form of resistance.

She sits on the sofa by the tea table, and I sit at her side. Her heart throbs, but without passion, her bosom rises and falls, but not in disquiet; occasionally she changes color, but in gradual transitions. Is that love? Not at all. She listens, she understands. She listens to the winged word, she understands it; she listens to another's speech, she understands it as her own; she listens to another's voice as it echoes within her, she understands this echo as if it were her own voice, making revelations to her and to another.

What am I doing? Do I delude her? By no means; to do so would avail me nothing. Do I steal her heart? By no means; I prefer, in any case, that the girl I love should retain her heart. Then what am I doing? I am creating for myself a heart in the likeness of her own. An artist paints his beloved, that is his delight; a sculptor carves his. This I also do, but in an intellectual sense. That I possess this image she does not know, and therein really lies my deception. Mysteriously I have secured it, and in this sense have I stolen her heart, just as Rebecca is said to have stolen Laban's heart when she craftily deprived him of his household gods.

Environment and setting do indeed influence one greatly; they belong to the elements that impress themselves most firmly and deeply on one's memory or rather on one's whole soul, so that they are never forgotten. However old I may become, it will never be possible for me to think of Cordelia among surroundings other than this little room. When I come to visit her, the maid admits me to the hall; Cordelia comes out of her own room, and as I open the door from the hall, she opens the other door, and at once our eyes meet. The living room is small and cozy and almost has the character of a cabinet. Although I have seen it from many different viewpoints, I am fondest of the view from the sofa. She sits there at my side; in front of us stands a round tea table, over which a tablecloth is spread in full folds. On the table stands a lamp shaped like a flower, which shoots up vigorously and luxuriantly to bear its crown, from which a delicately cut paper shade hangs down so lightly that it always trembles. The form of the lamp reminds me of the flora of oriental lands, the trembling

of the shade of the mild breezes in those regions. The floor is
covered with a carpet woven from a certain kind of osier, a
weave which at once betrays its foreign origin. Occasionally I let the lamp serve as the leading motive in my landscape.
Then I seem to half sit, half recline, on the ground with Cordelia beside me, under the flower formed by the lamp. At
other times I let the osier carpet evoke the idea of a ship, of
an officer's cabin. Then we sail far out on the ocean. Since we
sit far away from the window, we gaze directly into the
heaven's vast horizon. This helps to increase the illusion. When
I sit at her side, I summon up these pictures, which hasten just
as lightly over reality as death passes over one's grave.

Environment is always of great importance, particularly for
the sake of memory. Every erotic relation should be experienced in such a way that it will be easy to conjure up a picture
that possesses all its beauty. In order to do this successfully,
one must be especially observant of the surroundings. If one
does not find them to one's liking, they must be changed ac-
cordingly. In the case of Cordelia and her love, the environment is entirely suitable. How different is the picture I see
when I think of my little Emilie, and yet how suitable the environment was also in her case! I can visualize her only in the
little garden room. The doors stood open, a small garden in
front of the house restricted the view, forcing the eye to stop
there, to pause, before it boldly followed the road that vanished in the distance. Emilie was charming, but less significant
than Cordelia. The environment was in accordance with this.
The eye was held to the ground, it did not rush forward
boldly and impetuously, it rested on the small area of the foreground. The highway itself, although it disappeared romanti-
cally in the distance, did not allow the eye to roam beyond the
stretch directly in front of it, forcing the eye to return to the garden before it again traversed the same stretch. The room was
on the ground level. Cordelia's environment must have no fore-

ground, but only the horizon's infinite boldness. She must not be on the ground, she must glide; she must not walk, she must fly, not back and forth, but eternally forward.

When a man has become engaged, he is initiated most thoroughly into the follies of other engaged parties. A few days ago Licentiate Hansen turned up with the attractive young girl he is going to marry. He confided to me that she was charming, which I already knew, he confided to me that she was very young, which I also knew, and finally he confided to me that it was exactly for this reason that he had chosen her, so that he might shape her according to the ideal which had always hovered before him. Good Lord, what a pitiful licentiate—and what a healthy, blooming, cheerful girl! Now I am a fairly old practitioner, and yet I never approach a young girl otherwise than as nature's *Venerabile*, and from her I learn first. In so far as I can have any formative influence upon her, it is by teaching her again and again what I have learned from her.

Her soul must be moved and agitated in every possible direction, not, however, fragmentarily or sporadically, but totally. She must discover the infinite, she must experience that this is what lies closest to man. This she must discover, not by thought, which for her is the wrong way, but in imagination, which is the true mode of communication between her and me; for what is but a part with man, is the whole with woman. Not by following the strenuous way of thought shall she work toward the infinite, for woman is not born for toil, but she shall attain it by pursuing the easy way of the imagination and the heart. The infinite is just as natural for a young girl as the conception that all love must be happy. Wherever she turns, a young girl has the infinite about her, and the transition is a leap, but, *nota bene,* a feminine, not a masculine, leap. Why are men generally so clumsy? When a man is about to leap, he must first make lengthy preparations, measure the distance with his eye, and take several running starts; he loses heart and turns back again. At last he jumps and falls in. A young girl jumps in a different manner. In mountainous regions one often sees twin crags. A yawning abyss separates them, terrible to gaze down into. No man would dare this leap. A young girl, however, so the region's inhabitants say, did dare it, and therefore this place is called the Maiden's Leap. I readily believe it, just as I readily believe everything remarkable about a young girl, and it intoxicates me to hear the simple inhabitants talk about it. I believe everything, believe the marvelous, am amazed at it only in order to believe, for the only thing in the world that has truly amazed me is a young girl, it was the first thing and will be the last thing. And yet, for a young girl such a leap is but a hop, while a man's leap always becomes something ridiculous, because no matter how wide it strives to be, his exertion turns out to be as nothing in comparison with the distance between the crags, serving merely as a sort of measuring stick.

But who would be so foolish as to imagine a young girl taking a running start? One can indeed imagine her running, but this running is at the same time a game, an enjoyment, an unfolding of grace, whereas the conception of a running start separates what belongs together in a woman. The dialectical in a running start is contrary to woman's nature. And now the leap—who would want to be so crude here as to separate what belongs together? Her leap is a floating. And when she has reached the other side, she stands there, not exhausted from the effort, but more beautiful than ever, more soulful, she wafts a kiss over to us who stand on this side. Young, newborn, like a flower which has shot up from the root of the mountain, she sways over the abyss, so hazardously that everything nearly turns black before our eyes.

What she must learn is to make all the movements of infinity, to sway, to lose herself in moods, to confuse poetry and reality, truth and fiction, to revel in the infinite. When she has become familiar with this revelry, then I add the erotic, then she is what I want and desire her to be. Then is my service ended, my labor, then I take in all my sails; then I sit at her side, and it is under her sail that we move forward. In truth, when this girl begins to be erotically intoxicated, I shall have enough to do, while sitting by the rudder, to moderate the speed, so that nothing may happen prematurely or in an unattractive manner. Occasionally a small hole is made in the sail, and in the next moment we rush forward again.

In my uncle's house Cordelia grows more and more indignant. She has repeatedly requested that we should not return there, but her pleas avail nothing, I always have a new evasion ready. When we left there last night, she pressed my hand with unusual passion. Her stay there no doubt had been torture for her, and this is not surprising. If I did not always derive some amusement from watching the affectations of this artificial institution, I too, would find it intolerable. This morning I received a letter from her in which she poked fun at engagements with more wit than I had expected from her. I kissed the letter, it is the dearest one I have received from her. Very good, Cordelia, thus I wish it.

It is an odd coincidence that on Østergade there are two pastry shops directly opposite each other. On the second floor to the left lives a young woman. She usually hides behind a blind which screens the windowpane where she sits. The blind is made of very thin material, and whoever knows the girl or has seen her frequently will, if his eyesight is good, easily be able to recognize every feature, while to the person who does not know her or whose eyesight is poor, she will appear as a dark shadow. The latter to a certain degree applies to me, the former to a young officer who appears on the scene each day at 12 o'clock sharp, and raises his eyes to that blind. As a matter of fact, it was really the blind that attracted my attention to this beautiful telegraphic relation. The other windows have no blinds, and such a single blind covering only one windowpane usually indicates that a very retiring person is seated behind it.

One forenoon I was standing at the window of the pastry shop on the other side. It was precisely 12 o'clock. Without paying any attention to the passers-by, I fixed my eyes on that blind, and suddenly the dark shadow behind it began to move. A woman's head appeared in profile at the next pane, turning in a peculiar way in the direction toward which the blind faced. Thereupon the owner of this head nodded in a very friendly manner and again went into hiding behind the blind. In the first place, I deduced that the person she greeted was a man, for her greeting was too warm to be occasioned by the sight of a girl friend. In the second place, I deduced that the person for whom the greeting was intended generally came from the other side. She had, then, placed herself exactly right to be able to see him a long distance away, yes, even to greet him while she was concealed by the blind.—

Exactly as I had expected, at twelve o'clock sharp appears the hero in this little love scene, our dear lieutenant. I am sitting in the pastry shop on the ground floor of the house in which the young lady lives one flight up. The lieutenant has already fixed his eyes on her. Take care now, my dear fellow, it is not such an easy matter to greet gracefully up to the second floor. Incidentally, he isn't bad-looking, he is well built, erect, he has a good figure, an aquiline nose, black hair, his three-cornered hat is most becoming. But now problems arise. His knees begin to knock together, his legs become too long, they buckle under. It makes an impression on the eyes comparable to the feeling a man has when he suffers from a toothache and becomes overly conscious of the teeth in his mouth. If a

man concentrates all his power in his eyes and lifts them up to
the second floor, he easily draws too much strength from his
legs. I beg your pardon, Lieutenant, for intercepting this glance
in its heavenward flight! It is an impertinence, I know it well
enough. One cannot call this glance very meaningful, on the
contrary, it is rather meaningless, and yet it is very promising.
But these many promises seem to rise too strongly to his head;
he totters, to use the poet's word about Agnete, he reels, he
falls. That is cruel, and could I have had my way, it would
never have happened. He is too good for that. It is really most
embarrassing, for if a man wishes to impress the ladies as a
cavalier, he must never fall. If one wishes to be a cavalier, he
must pay attention to such matters. If, on the other hand, the
accent is on the intellect, then such matters are unimportant.
One sinks into oneself, one slumps, and if one actually falls,
it is an action that attracts no attention at all.

What impression may this incident have made upon my
little lady? It is a pity that I cannot be on both sides of this
Hellespont at the same time. To be sure, I could post an acquaintance on the other side of the street, but, for one thing,
I always prefer to make my own observations, for another, it
is impossible to tell what there may be in this business for me.
In such a case it is well never to have a confidant, since then
one must waste a great deal of time drawing him out and
confusing him about the matter.

I am really getting tired of my good lieutenant. Day after
day he struts by in full uniform. Such constancy is terrifying.
Is such conduct becoming to a soldier? Sir, don't you carry side
arms? Ought you not to take the house by storm and ravish the
girl? Now if you were a student, a licentiate, a curate who
lives on hope, that would be a different matter. Still, I forgive
you, for the girl pleases me the more I gaze at her. She is
pretty, her brown eyes are full of mischief. When she is awaiting your arrival, her mien is transfigured by a higher beauty,

indescribably becoming to her. From that I infer that she must
have a great deal of imagination, and imagination is the natural rouge of the fair sex.

My Cordelia!

What is longing? Our language and our poets rhyme it with
the word for prison. How preposterous! * As if only a prisoner
could feel longing! As if one could not feel longing when one is
free! Assuming I were free, would I not long? And on the other
side, I am free, yes, free as a bird, and yet how full of longing
I am! I long when I go to you, I long when I leave you; even
when I sit beside you, I long for you. But can one long for
what one has? Yes, when one considers that in the very next
moment one may no longer have it. My longing is an eternal
impatience. Not until I had lived through all eternities and
assured myself that at every moment you belonged to me, not
until then would I return to you and live with you through all
eternities, and even then I would not have patience enough to
be separated from you for a single moment without longing,
but security enough to sit quietly at your side.

Your Johannes

My Cordelia!

Outside the door stands a small cabriolet which to me seems
larger than the whole world, since it is large enough for two;
drawn by a pair of horses, wild and unmanageable as the

* The words *laengsel*, "longing," and *faengsel*, "prison," form a rhyme.
The use of the word *unrimelig*, "preposterous," "absurd," involves a pun,
its stem syllable being *rim*, "rhyme." Cf. the German word *ungereimt*.

forces of nature, impatient as my passions, intrepid as your thoughts. If you are willing, I shall carry you away, my Cordelia! Do you command it? Your command is the signal that loosens the reins and releases the joy of flight. I carry you away, not from some human beings to others, but out of the world.

The horses rear, the carriage leaves the ground, they rise up vertically, almost above our heads. We drive into the azure through the clouds; a roaring sound accompanies us. Is it we who are sitting still while all the world is moving, or is it our bold flight that is in motion? Do you feel dizzy, my Cordelia? Then hold fast to me. I do not grow dizzy. One's mind never grows dizzy when one thinks of one thing only, and I think only of you—nor does one's body when one fixes one's eyes on one object only, and I look only at you. Hold fast! If the world came to an end, if our light carriage vanished beneath us, we would still hold each other close, soaring in the harmony of the spheres.

Your Johannes

This is almost too much. My servant has been waiting for six hours and I have been waiting for two, in rain and wind, just to waylay that dear child, Charlotte Hahn. She is in the habit of visiting an old aunt of hers every Wednesday afternoon between two and five. But today, just when I am particularly anxious to meet her, she doesn't turn up. And why do I want to meet her? Because she puts me in a very definite mood. I greet her, she nods in a manner at once indescribably earthly and yet divine. She almost stops, it is as if she were about to sink into the ground, and yet she has a soulful look as if she were about to be lifted up to heaven. When I gaze at her, my thoughts grow at once lofty and yet desirous. For the rest, the girl does not occupy my mind at all. All I want is this greeting, nothing more, provided she gives it voluntarily. Her greeting creates a mood in me, and this mood I then squander on Cordelia.

I'm inclined to believe that in some way she has given us the slip. It is not only in comedies but also in real life that it is difficult to waylay a young girl; one needs to have more than one pair of eyes. There once was a nymph, Cardea, who devoted herself to fooling men. She lived in a wood, lured her lovers into the densest thickets, and then disappeared. She tried to fool Janus also, but he fooled her, for he had eyes at the back of his head.

My letters do not fail of their purpose. They develop her emotionally, but not erotically. For the latter purpose *billets* rather than letters should be employed. The more the erotic then comes to the fore, the shorter they will become, but the more securely they will enfold the erotic center. However, in order to prevent her from becoming sentimental or soft, irony will again be used to harden her feelings, but at the same time it will make her eager for the nourishment dearest to her. The *billets* will suggest the highest remotely and vaguely. As soon as this presentiment begins to dawn in her soul, the relation will be broken off. Due to my influence the presentiment then takes form in her soul as if it were her own thought, her own heart's impulse. It is that, and that only, I want.

My Cordelia!

Somewhere in this city there lives a little family consisting of a widow and three daughters. Two of these go to the Royal Kitchen to learn to cook. It was about five o'clock one spring afternoon. The door to the living room is opened gently, a spying glance steals about the room. It is empty but for a young girl sitting at the piano. The door is ajar, so one can listen unobserved. It is no artist who is playing, otherwise the door would be shut tight. She is playing a Swedish song, which tells of the transitoriness of youth and beauty. The words mock the girl's youth and beauty; the girl's youth and beauty mock the words. Which is right, the girl or the words? The tones sound so soft, so melancholy, as if sadness were the arbitrator who should decide the dispute.—But it is wrong, this melancholy. What connection is there between youth and these reflections? What fellowship between morning and evening? The keys tremble and quiver; the spirits of the sounding board rise in confusion and do not understand one another—my Cordelia, why so intense, to what end this passion!

How far back in time must an event be for us to remember it, how far back so that memory's longing can no longer grasp it? Most people have a limit in this respect; whatever lies too near them in time they cannot remember, likewise not, whatever lies too far away from them. I know no limit. What was experienced yesterday I thrust back a thousand years in time and remember as if it had been experienced yesterday.

Your Johannes

My Cordelia!

A secret I have to confide to you, my confidante. To whom should I confide it? To the echo? It would betray it. To the stars? They are cold. To people? They do not understand it. Only to you dare I confide it, for you know how to keep it. There is a girl more beautiful than my soul's dream, purer than the light of the sun, deeper than the sea's source, prouder than the eagle's flight—there is a girl—oh, incline your head to my head and to my words, so that my secret may slip into it! This girl I love more than my life, for she is my life, more than all my desires, for she is my sole desire, more than all my thoughts, for she is my sole thought, more warmly than the sun loves the flower, more ardently than sorrow loves the secrecy of the troubled spirit, more longingly than the desert's burning sands love the rain. To her I attach myself more tenderly than the mother's eye to her child, more trustingly than the worshiper's soul to God, more inseparably than the plant to its root.

Your head becomes heavy and thoughtful, it sinks down on your breast, your bosom rises in support—my Cordelia! You have understood me, you have understood me exactly, to the letter, no tittle has escaped you. Shall I attune my ears and let your voice assure me of this? Or is there occasion to doubt? Will you keep this secret? Dare I depend on you? They tell about men who because of terrible crimes pledged one another to mutual silence. To you I have entrusted a secret which is my life and my life's content—have you nothing to trust to me that is so significant, so beautiful, so chaste, that supernatural forces would awake if it were betrayed?

Your Johannes

My Cordelia!

The sky is overcast—it draws together dark rain clouds as a scowling countenance knits dark brows. The trees in the forest sway, tossed about by unquiet dreams. I have lost you in the forest. Behind every tree I see a feminine being resembling you, but whenever I come nearer, it hides behind the next tree. Will you not reveal yourself to me, appear as one being? Everything becomes confused before me; the individual parts of the forest lose their outlines, I behold all about me a foggy sea, where everywhere feminine forms resembling you appear and vanish. I do not see you, you move constantly in a sea of contemplation, and yet each separate likeness of you suffices to render me happy. What is the reason for this—is it your being's rich unity or my being's poor multiplicity?—Is loving you not tantamount to loving a world?

Your Johannes

I should find it most interesting, if it were possible, to record exactly the conversations I carry on with Cordelia. But that, it is easy to realize, is an impossibility. Even if I managed to recall every single word exchanged between us, the attempt would fail, as it could not convey the element of simultaneity, which really forms the nerve center of the conversation, the surprised outburst, the passionateness, which is its life principle. In general I have, of course, not prepared myself for our talks, since to do so would be contrary to the very nature of conversation, particularly erotic conversation. On the other hand, I constantly have *in mente* the contents of my letters, just as I constantly have before my eyes the moods these may call forth in her. Naturally it would never occur to me to ask her whether she had read my letter. That she has done so, I can easily ascertain. I never talk with her directly about it, but I maintain a mysterious communication with it in the course of my conversations, partly to fix one or another impression more deeply in her soul, partly to wrest it from her and make her irresolute. Then she can reread the letter and gain a new impression of it, and so on.

A change has taken place in her and is still taking place in her. If I were to describe the condition of her soul at this moment, I should designate it as pantheistic daring. Her glance reveals this immediately. It is daring, almost foolhardy in expectancy, as if at every moment it demanded and was prepared to behold the extraordinary. Like an eye that sees beyond itself, so this glance sees beyond that which appears immediately before it and beholds the marvelous. It is daring, almost foolhardy in expectancy, but not in self-confidence; it is therefore somewhat dreamy and pleading, not proud and commanding. She seeks the marvelous outside herself, she seems to pray for it to appear, as if it were not in her own power to evoke it. This must be prevented, otherwise I get the upper hand of her too soon.

Yesterday she said to me that there was something regal in my nature. Perhaps she wants to humble herself, but that will not do at all. Certainly, dear Cordelia, there is something regal in my nature, but you do not suspect what kind of a realm I rule over. It is the realm of stormy moods. Like Aeolus I hold them shut up in the mountain of my personality and let now one, now another, escape. Flattery will give her self-esteem; the difference between mine and thine will be made valid; everything will be transferred to her side. Great caution is needed in the use of flattery. At times one must set oneself very high, yet so that there remains a still higher place; at other times one must set oneself very low. The first is more correct when one is moving toward the intellectual, the second, when one is moving toward the erotic.

Does she owe me anything? Nothing at all. Could I wish that she did? By no means. I am too much the connoisseur, I have too much understanding of the erotic for such foolishness. If this were really the case, I should endeavor with all my might to get her to forget it and lull my own thoughts about it to sleep. With respect to the labyrinth of her heart, every young girl is an Ariadne; she possesses the thread by which

one can find one's way through it, but she possesses it in such
a way that she herself does not know how to use it.

My Cordelia!

Speak—I obey. Your wish is a command. Your prayer is an
omnipotent conjuration, every fleeting wish of yours is a kind-
ness toward me; for I obey you not as a ministering spirit, as
if I stood outside of you. When you command, then your will
grows, and with it also I; for I am a confusion of the soul
which but awaits a word from you.

Your Johannes

My Cordelia!

You know that I am very fond of talking to myself. I have
found myself to be the most interesting person among my acquaintances. Sometimes I feared that I might finally run out of
subjects for these conversations; now I am without fear, now I
have you. And so I now and forevermore talk to myself about
you, about the most interesting subject to the most interesting
man—alas, for I am only an interesting person, you the most
interesting subject.

Your Johannes

My Cordelia!

It seems to you that I have loved you but a very short time,
and so you seem to fear that I may have been in love before.

There are manuscripts where the keen eye at once senses the presence of an older script, which in the course of time has been supplanted by insignificant, foolish material. By means of acids the later script is obliterated, and now the original stands out plain and clear. Thus your eye has taught me to find myself in myself; I let forgetfulness consume everything which is not concerned with you, and then I discover an ancient, a divinely young, original script, then I discover that my love for you is just as old as I am.

Your Johannes

My Cordelia!

How can a kingdom stand which is divided against itself? How shall I be able to survive, when I am divided against myself? About what? About you, in order, if possible, to find rest in the thought that I am in love with you. But how shall I find this rest? One of the contending powers will again and again seek to persuade the other that it is most deeply and tenderly in love; in the next moment the other side will do the same. It would not distress me greatly if the contest were waged on the outside, if there were someone who dared to be in love with you, or dared to stop being so—the crime is equally great. But this contest within myself consumes me, this one passion in its doubleness.

Your Johannes

Just disappear, my little fisher maiden, just go and hide among the trees! But first pick up your burden, it is becoming to you to bend down. Yes, at this very moment you arch your body with a natural grace under the bundle of brushwood you have gathered. That such a creature should bear such a burden! Like a dancer you reveal the beauty of your forms—you have a slender waist, a full bosom, a voluptuous build; every recruiting officer cannot but agree with that. You believe perhaps that these charms are trivialities, it seems to you that the ladies of society are far more beautiful. Alas, my child! You do not know how much deception there is in the world.

Just continue on your way with your load into the vast forest, which probably stretches for many, many miles into the country as far as the barrier of the blue mountains. Perhaps you are not a real fisher maiden, but an enchanted princess; perhaps you serve a troll; he is cruel enough to make you fetch firewood in the forest. It is always thus in fairy tales. Why would you go deeper into the woods otherwise? If you were really a fisher maiden, you would go down to the fishing village with your faggots, past me who linger on the other side of the road.

Just pursue the footpath which winds playfully among the trees, my eyes find you; just keep looking back at me, my eyes follow you. Move me you cannot, desire does not draw me from the fence on which I sit calmly, smoking my cigar. Some other time—perhaps. Yes, your glance is roguish indeed, when you half turn back your head; your light step is alluring —yes, I know it, I understand where this path leads—to the solitude of the forest, to the murmuring trees, to the many-voiced stillness. Look, even the sky favors you, it hides away in the clouds, it darkens the background of the forest, it is as if it drew the curtains for us.—Farewell, my pretty fisher maiden, live well. Thanks for your favor, it was a lovely moment, a mood, not strong enough to induce me to leave my place on the fence, but still rich in inner emotion.

———

When Jacob had bargained with Laban about payment for his services, when they had agreed that Jacob should watch the white sheep and as a reward for his work should have all the ring-straked and speckled lambs which were born in Laban's flock, then he laid rods in the gutters in the watering troughs and let the sheep look at them. Thus I place myself everywhere before Cordelia, her eyes behold me constantly. It strikes her as sheer attentiveness on my part; I for my part, however, know that her soul thereby is losing interest in everything else, that there is being developed in her a mental concupiscence which sees me everywhere.

My Cordelia!

As if I could ever forget you! Is my love, then, a work of memory? Even if time erased everything else from its tablets, even if it destroyed memory itself, my relation to you would remain alive, you would still not be forgotten. As if I could forget you! What would I remember then? I have even forgotten myself in order to remember you; if I did forget you, I would come to remember myself, but at the very moment I remembered myself, I would have to remember you again. As if I could forget you! What would happen if I did?

There is a picture dating from ancient times. It represents Ariadne. She is leaping up from her couch and gazing anxiously toward a ship departing under full sail. By her side stands Cupid with unstrung bow, drying his eyes. Behind her stands a winged and helmeted female figure. It is generally assumed that this figure represents Nemesis. Imagine this picture, imagine it slightly changed. Cupid does not weep, and his bow is not unstrung. Or would you then have become less beautiful, less victorious, because I had grown mad? Cupid smiles and draws his bow. Nemesis does not stand inactive at your side, she also draws her bow. In that picture we see on the ship the figure of a man who is busy working. We assume

that it is Theseus. Not so in my picture. He stands on the
stern, he looks back longingly, he stretches out his arms, he
has repented, or, rather, his madness has left him, but the ship
carries him away. Cupid and Nemesis both aim at him, arrows
fly from both bows, they do not swerve; one senses that they
will both hit the same place in his heart as a sign that his love
was the avenging nemesis.

Your Johannes

My Cordelia!

People say that I am in love with myself. That doesn't surprise me, for how could they notice that I am able to love, since
I love only you; how should anyone suspect it, since I love only
you? I am in love with myself, why? Because I am in love with
you, for I truly love you, you alone, and everything which belongs to you, and so I love myself, because this myself belongs
to you. Hence, if I ceased to love you, I would cease to love
myself. What in the profane eyes of the world is an expression
of the greatest egoism is in your initiated sight an expression of
the purest sympathy; what in the profane eyes of the world is
an expression of the most prosaic self-preservation is in your
hallowed sight an expression of the most exuberant self-
destruction.

Your Johannes

What I feared most was that the whole development might
last overlong. I see, however, that Cordelia is making such
great progress that it becomes necessary to set everything in
motion in order to keep her fully involved. Not for all the

world must she become weary before the time, that is to say, before that time when time is past for her.

When people are in love, they do not follow the highroad. It is only married couples whom one encounters in the middle of the king's highway. When lovers go walking from Nøddebo, they do not pass along Esrom Lake, although the way there is really only a hunter's path, but it is a cleared way, and love prefers to clear its own ways. They penetrate deeper into Gribsskov. And when thus they wander arm in arm through the forest, they understand each other, and many things which before were obscurely risible and embarrassing are clarified. They do not suspect that someone is present.

Well then, this beautiful beech tree became a witness to your love, under its crown you confessed your love for the first time. You remembered everything so vividly, the first time you saw each other, the first time you held hands while dancing, the first time you took leave of each other toward the early morning, when neither of you would confess your feelings to yourself, let alone to the other.—It is entertaining indeed to listen to these amorous recitals.—They fell on their knees under the tree, they pledged each other lasting love, they sealed the pact with the first kiss.—These are fruitful moods to be lavished on Cordelia.

This beech, then, became a witness. Oh yes, a tree is a suitable witness, but still, it is not enough. No doubt you think that heaven was also a witness, but heaven, just heaven, is a very abstract idea. Well, this is why there was another witness present.

Should I rise and let them notice that I am here? No, perhaps they know me, and then the game would be ruined. Should I, as they are leaving, rise and give them to understand that another person was present? No, that is inexpedient. Let silence reign over their secret—as long as I wish. They are in my power, I can separate them whenever I will. I am wise to

their secret; only from him or from her can I have learned it
—from her, that is impossible—consequently from him, that
is detestable. Bravo! And yet this is well-nigh malign. Well, I
shall see. If I cannot get a definite impression of her normally,
as I would prefer, then I have no choice in the matter.

My Cordelia!

Poor I am—you are my wealth; gloomy I am—you are my
light. I possess nothing, need nothing. And how could I possess
anything? It is a contradiction to say that he can own something who does not own himself. I am as happy as a child that
can and need own nothing. I own nothing, for I belong only to
you; I am not, I have ceased to be, in order to be yours.

Your Johannes

My Cordelia!

Mine, what does this word denote? Not what belongs to me,
but what I belong to, what contains my whole being, which is
mine insofar as I belong to it. My God, after all, is not the
God who belongs to me, but the God to whom I belong, and
the same holds true when I say my native land, my home, my
calling, my longing, my hope. If heretofore there had been no
immortality, then would this thought, that I am yours, break
through nature's customary course.

Your Johannes

My Cordelia!

What am I? The modest narrator who follows your triumphs,
the dancer who crouches beneath you while you leap up with

graceful agility; the branch on which you rest for a moment when you are tired from flying; the bass voice which lends support to the soprano voice's ecstasy, enabling it to rise still higher.—What am I? I am the gravitational force which holds you to the earth. What am I then? Body, mass, earth, dust, and ashes—you, my Cordelia, you are soul and spirit.

Your Johannes

My Cordelia!

Love is everything. Hence for the one who loves, everything has ceased to have meaning and acquires meaning only from the interpretation love puts upon it. If a fiancé were found out to be concerned about another girl, he would probably stand there like a criminal and his intended would be highly indignant. You, on the contrary—this I know—would see an act of homage in such an admission, for you know that it is an impossibility that I should love another. It is my love for you that casts reflected splendor over the whole of life. When I am concerned about someone else, it is not for the purpose of proving to myself that I love not her, but only you—that would be presumptuous; but since my whole soul is filled with you, life takes on another meaning for me. It becomes a myth about you.

Your Johannes

My Cordelia!

My love consumes me, only my voice remains, a voice which has fallen in love with you, which everywhere whispers to you that I love you. Oh, does it tire you to hear this voice? Everywhere it surrounds you; in the same manifold, unsteady manner my reflecting soul encompasses your pure, deep being.

Your Johannes

My Cordelia!

One reads in olden tales that a river fell in love with a maiden. My soul is like a river that loves you. Now it is quiet and reflects your image deeply and without movement; now it imagines that it has captured your image, then its waves surge up to prevent your escaping; at times its surface ripples gently and plays with your image; at other times it has lost it, then its waves become black and despairing.—Thus is my soul: like a river which has become enamored of you.

Your Johannes

To be quite frank: without possessing a particularly vivid imagination, one could conceive of a conveyance that is pleasanter, more comfortable, and above all, more consistent with one's station in life; to ride with a peat cutter creates a stir only in a figurative sense.—In a pinch, however, one gratefully accepts a lift. One goes out on the highway for a stretch, one climbs onto a cart, one rides a mile without meeting anyone; two miles, all goes well; one begins to feel calm and safe. The surrounding country looks better from this level than from the ground. One has covered almost three miles—now who would have expected to encounter a Copenhagener out here on the highway? One can tell that he is a Copenhagener, and not a rustic, from his characteristic gaze, so keen, so observant, so appraising, and a little mocking.

Yes, dear girl, your position is anything but comfortable.

You sit there as if you were being presented on a salver; the wagon is flat, there is no recess for your feet. Well, it is your own fault; my carriage is entirely at your service; I venture to offer you a far less embarrassing place, provided it doesn't embarrass you to sit at my side. Should this be the case, I'll turn over the whole carriage to you and occupy the driver's seat, pleased at being permitted to take you to your destination.—The straw hat does not adequately protect you against lateral glances. It is useless for you to lower your head, I can still admire your lovely profile.

Is it not annoying that the peasant salutes me? But a peasant should always salute a gentleman. Do not imagine that you can escape that easily. Here is a tavern, a station, as it were, and a peat cutter is too devout a man not to stop here for a little prayer. Now I shall concern myself with him. I have an uncommon talent for pleasing peat cutters. Oh, may I also succeed in pleasing you! He cannot resist my offer, and when he has accepted it, then he cannot resist its effect. If I cannot influence him, then my servant can.—Now he goes into the taproom, leaving you alone on the wagon in the shed.

Heaven only knows who the girl may be! Could she be a little middle-class maiden, perhaps a parish clerk's daughter? For a parish clerk's daughter she is uncommonly pretty and unusually well dressed. That clerk must have a good living. It occurs to me that she may be a little blueblood who is tired of riding in her equipage; perhaps she is hiking out to the country villa and hopes to become involved in a little adventure on the way. It is quite possible, such things do happen.—The peasant knows nothing, he is a blockhead who knows only how to drink. Well, let him drink, he is welcome to it.

But what do I see? It is neither more nor less than Miss Jespersen, Hansine Jespersen, a daughter of the wholesaler in town. Heaven preserve me, we two know each other. I met her once on Bredgade, she was sitting with her back to the horses and could not get the carriage window up. I put on my glasses and had the pleasure of following her with my eyes. It was a very embarrassing position; there were so many in the carriage that she could not move, but apparently she did not dare to protest. Her present position is just as embarrassing. It is clear that we two are meant for each other. She must be a very romantic little girl, and she is definitely out on her own.

There comes my servant with the peat cutter. He is dead drunk. How disgusting! They are a depraved lot, these peat cutters. Alas, yes! And yet there are worse people than peat cutters.—See, now you are up against it! Now you will have to drive the horses yourself, it is quite romantic.—You refuse my invitation, you insist that you are a very good driver. You don't fool me, I notice very well how cunning you are. When you have followed the highway a little while, you will stop and get down. It is easy to find a hiding-place in the woods.

My horse shall be saddled. I shall follow on horseback.— Look, now I am ready, now you may feel safe against any attack.—Do not become so terribly frightened, or I shall turn back at once. I merely wanted to frighten you a little in order to provide you with an occasion for heightening your natural beauty. You do not know that it was I who got the peasant drunk, and I have not addressed a single improper word to you. Everything may yet become all right; I shall not fail to give the affair such a turn that you will be able to laugh at the whole story. All I desire is a little settling of accounts with you. Do not believe that I ever try to take a girl by surprise. I am a friend of freedom, and whatever I cannot get on a voluntary basis holds no interest for me.

"Surely you see for yourself that it will not be possible for you to continue the excursion in this manner. I myself am going hunting, that is why I am on horseback. My carriage and horses are ready at the tavern. If you command, my carriage will be here in a moment and take you wherever you wish. Unfortunately I cannot have the pleasure of accompanying you, for I am bound by a hunting commitment, and that is sacred."

You accept. In a moment everything will be in order.—Now you see that you do not need to be embarrassed when you see me again, or, at least, not more so than is becoming to you. You can be amused at the whole business, laugh a little, and think a little about me. More I do not ask. This may seem little, but for me it is enough. It is the beginning, and I am especially strong where beginning elements are involved.

Last evening there was a small social gathering at the aunt's place. I knew that Cordelia would take out her knitting things. I therefore had hid a note among them. She dropped it, picked it up, was moved, and had a yearning look. One must always make use of such situations; incredible advantages are often gained in this way. An essentially insignificant note, read under such circumstances, becomes infinitely significant to her. She didn't get a chance to talk with me; I had arranged it so that I had to accompany a lady home. She therefore had to wait until today. Such a device permits the impression to penetrate more deeply into her soul. She feels that I am being attentive all the time, and the advantage I gain is that I am being installed everywhere in her thoughts, that I surprise her everywhere.

Love indeed has its own dialectic. Once I was in love with a young girl. Last summer I saw an actress in a Dresden theater who strikingly resembled her. I therefore wished to make her acquaintance, which I succeeded in doing, but the upshot was that I discovered that the dissimilarity was rather great. Today I met a lady on the street who reminded me of that actress. This story can continue endlessly.

Everywhere my thoughts encompass Cordelia, I post them

about her like angels. As Venus rides in her chariot drawn by doves, so Cordelia sits in her triumphal chariot, to which my thoughts are harnessed like winged creatures. She sits there joyous, rich as a child, almighty as a goddess. I walk at her side. Truly a young girl is and remains the *Venerabile* of nature and the whole of existence. There is no one who knows this better than myself. The only pity is that this glory is of such short duration. She smiles at me, she greets me, she waves to me as if she were my sister. A glance reminds her that she is my beloved.

Love has many positions. Cordelia is making good progress. She sits on my lap, her arm, soft and warm, encircles my neck; she leans against my breast, lightly, without bodily weight. Her soft forms hardly touch me, like a flower her lovely figure twines about me, freely like a ribbon. Her eyes are hidden under their lids, her bosom is dazzlingly white like snow, so smooth that my eye cannot rest there, it would glance off if her bosom did not heave. What does this agitation mean? Is it love? Perhaps. It is its anticipation, its dream. It still lacks energy. She embraces me diffusely, as it were, as the cloud embraces the transfigured one, lightly as a breeze, tenderly as one holds a flower. She kisses me vaguely, as the sky kisses the sea, gently and quietly as the dew kisses the flower, solemnly as the sea kisses the moon's reflection.

At this moment I should call her passion a naive passion. When the tide has turned, and I begin to withdraw in earnest, then she will muster everything in order truly to enchain me. She has no means for this other than the erotic, but this will now appear on a totally different scale. It becomes a weapon in her hand which she wields against me. I shall then have the reflected passion. She fights for her own sake, because she knows that I possess the erotic; she fights for her own sake in order to overcome me. She herself feels the need for a higher form of the erotic. What I taught her to surmise by inflaming her, my coldness now teaches her to understand, but in such a way that she believes she is discovering it herself. By means of it she seeks to take me by surprise; she wants to believe that she has surpassed me in boldness and thus has caught me. Her passion then becomes definite, energetic, reasoning, dialectic, her kiss total, her embrace without hiatus.—In me she seeks her freedom; the more firmly I encompass her, the more easily she finds it. The engagement collapses. When this happens, she will require a little rest, so that nothing unaesthetic will appear in this wild tumult. Her passion regains new strength, and she is mine.

Just as in the time of Edvard of blessed memory I took care of her reading indirectly, so now I do it directly. I provide her with the literature I regard as the best nourishment: mythology and fairy tales. Still, she has her freedom in this as in everything else. I draw everything out of her. If it is not there already, then I implant it.

When the servant girls go to the Deer Park in summer, it generally turns out to be a sorry entertainment. They go there only once a year, and therefore they feel that they ought to get something out of it. So they put on hat and shawl and disfigure themselves in every way. Their gaiety is wild, unattractive, and lascivious. No, I much prefer Frederiksberg Park. They go there on Sunday afternoon, and so do I. Everything there is proper and respectable, the gaiety itself is quieter and more refined.

Surely the man who has no appreciation of servant girls loses a great deal thereby. Their vast number really provides the finest militia we have in Denmark. If I were king, I know what I would do—it certainly would not be reviewing the troops of the line. If I were one of the city's thirty-two aldermen, I should immediately move that a welfare committee be appointed whose task it would be, in every possible way, by insight, advice, admonition, and suitable rewards, to encourage the servant girls to make a careful and attractive toilette. Why should beauty go to waste, why should it pass through life unnoticed? Let it show itself at its finest at least once a week! But above all let us have taste and restraint. A servant girl ought not to look like a lady—in this respect the *Police Gazette* is quite right, but the reasons stated by this highly respected sheet in support of its opinion are entirely fallacious. If it were possible to effect so desirable a flowering of the girls of the servant class, would this in turn not have a beneficial effect upon the daughters in our homes? Or am I being too daring when I descry a future for Denmark which may truly be called nonpareil? If I should be so fortunate as to be still alive when this golden age comes, I could employ the whole day with a good conscience walking about in the highways and byways and feasting my eyes. How my thoughts do roam, how bold, how patriotic they are! But I forget, I am taking a stroll in Frederiksberg Park, where the servant girls turn up on Sunday afternoon and I as well.

First come the peasant girls, hand in hand with their sweethearts, or, in another pattern, all the girls hand in hand in front, all the young fellows behind, or, in still another pattern, two girls and one young fellow. This crowd forms the frame, they like to stand or sit along the trees in the large square in front of the pavilion. They are healthy, fresh, only the color contrasts are a little too strong, both with regard to their complexion and their clothing. Next there appear, within this frame, the girls from Jutland and Funen. They are tall and straight, their build a bit too sturdy, their dress a bit careless. Here the committee would find plenty to do. Representatives of the Bornholm division are also present: clever cooks, but not very approachable either in the kitchen or in Frederiksberg Park; their manner has something proudly forbidding. Their presence therefore is not without effect because of the contrast, I should miss them if they did not turn up, but I rarely have anything to do with them.

Now come the troops of the center, the girls from Nyboder. Of moderate height, plump, full-bosomed, with a delicate complexion, gay, happy, lively, talkative, a little given to coquetry, and above all, bareheaded. Their apparel may greatly resemble that of a lady, but two things should be observed: they do not wear a shawl but a kerchief, and they have no hat—at most, a smart little cap, but preferably they are bareheaded.

Well, look who is here! Good day to you, Marie! What a surprise to meet you here! It is a long time since I saw you last. I suppose you are still in service at the Councillor's?

"Yes."

It is a very good position, is it not?

"Yes."

But you seem to be all alone out here. Is there no one with you? Your sweetheart? Perhaps he is busy today, or are you waiting for him? What, you are not engaged? Impossible! The prettiest girl in Copenhagen, a girl who is in service at the Councillor's, who is a credit and an example to all servant girls, a girl who knows how to dress so neatly and . . . so richly! What a dainty handkerchief you are holding in your hand, of the finest cambric and with an embroidered hem. I'll wager it cost ten kroner. Surely many a fine lady does not own the like . . . and French gloves . . . and a silk parasol . . . And such a girl would not be engaged? Why, it's absurd! If I remember correctly, Jens was quite fond of you. You know whom I mean, Jens, the servant of the merchant on the third floor . . . I see I wasn't mistaken . . . Well, why didn't you become engaged? Jens was a handsome fellow, he had a good position, and with the merchant's help he would no doubt eventually have become a policeman or a fireman. It wouldn't have been a bad match at all . . . It must have been your fault, you were too hard on him.

"No, but I found out that Jens had been engaged to a girl
once before, and I was told that he didn't treat her right at
all."

You don't say so! Who would have believed that Jens was
such a scoundrel . . . yes, those guardsmen, they are not to be
depended on. You did the right thing, a girl like you is far too
good for Tom, Dick, and Harry. You will make a much better
match some day, I promise you that . . .

How is Miss Juliana? I have not seen her for a long time.
Surely my pretty Marie could let me have some news of her.
Just because one has been unhappy in love oneself, one doesn't
have to be indifferent toward the sufferings of others . . . There
are so many people here, I dare not talk with you about
it, I am afraid someone may try to eavesdrop . . . Listen just
for a moment, my pretty Marie. Ah, here is the right spot, here
in this shaded walk, where the trees form a tangled mass
that hides us from others, where we see nobody, where we
hear no human voice, nothing but the soft echo of the music,
here I dare speak of my secret . . . Is it not true, if Jens had
not turned out to be a bad fellow, you would now be walking
with him here, arm in arm, you would be listening to the joyous music and reveling in an even greater joy? . . . Why are
you so moved? Do forget Jens . . . Will you then be unjust to
me? It was to meet you that I came out here, it was to see you
that I used to go to the Councillor's. You must have noticed
that. Whenever it was possible, I stole away to the kitchen
door . . . You must be mine . . . We shall have the banns published from the pulpit . . . Tomorrow evening I shall explain
everything to you . . . up the backstairs, the door to the left,
directly opposite the kitchen door . . . Goodbye, my pretty
Marie, let no one know that you have seen me here or spoken
with me, you know my secret now . . .

She is lovely indeed, something might really be made of her.
—Once I get a foothold in her bedchamber, I myself shall proclaim the banns from the pulpit. I have always sought to de-

velop the beautiful Greek ideal of αὐτάρχεια and especially to
dispense with the services of a parson.

It might prove very interesting if it were possible for me to
stand behind Cordelia when she receives a letter from me.
Then I could easily find out to what extent she assimilates
my letters erotically in the truest sense of that word. On the
whole, letters are, and will always continue to be, an invaluable means of making an impression upon a young girl; the
dead letter often has far greater influence than the living word.
A letter is a mysterious communication; one is master of the
situation, one feels no pressure from anyone's presence, and I
believe that a young girl wants nothing more than to be all
alone with her ideal, at least at certain moments, and it is
precisely at these moments that the ideal exerts the strongest
influence upon her mind. Even if her ideal seems to have
found an ever so complete expression in a definite beloved
object, there are still moments when she feels that the ideal
possesses an extravagance lacking in reality. These great feasts
of the atonement must be vouchsafed her; only one must
take care to make correct use of them, so that she does not return from them to reality weakened, but strengthened. Letters
help to bring this about, since through them one is present
spiritually, although invisible, in these holy moments of conse-
cration, while the idea that the living person is the author of
the letter makes possible a natural and easy transition to
reality.

Could I become jealous of Cordelia? Hell and damnation,
yes! And yet, in another sense, no! For if I saw that her nature
became unsettled and not as I desired it to be, even though I
was winning in my fight against the other, I would abandon
her.

An ancient philosopher has said that if one were to write

down accurately everything he experiences, then he would be
a philosopher without knowing anything about philosophy. I
have now lived in close association with the community of the
affianced for a considerable period of time. Such a connection
must eventually bear fruit. I have therefore considered collect-
ing material for a book entitled *Contribution to the Theory of
the Kiss*, dedicated to all tender lovers. By the way, it is
strange that no monograph on this subject exists. If, then, I
succeed in completing the work, I shall also be remedying a
long-felt want. Could it be that this lack of literature results
from the failure on the part of the philosophers to concern
themselves with such matters or from their failure to understand them?

In the meantime I am able to offer several hints. The complete kiss requires a girl and a man as active participants. A
kiss between men is tasteless, or, what is worse, distasteful. I
believe, furthermore, that a kiss comes nearer the abstract idea
when a man kisses a girl than when a girl kisses a man. When
in the course of years there has developed an indifference in
the man-woman relation, the kiss has lost its significance. This
is true of the connubial domestic kiss with which married people wipe each other's mouth clean, in lieu of a napkin, when
they have reached the end of a meal.

If the difference in age is very great, the kiss is outside the
idea. I remember that the senior class in a girl's school in one
of the provinces used a peculiar expression, "to kiss the King's
Counsel," a phrase which for them had only unpleasant con-
notations. The origin of this expression was as follows: the
schoolmistress had a brother-in-law who lived in her house, had
been a king's counsel, was an older man, and therefore thought
he was entitled to the privilege of kissing the young girls.

The kiss must be the expression of a definite passion. When
a brother and a sister who are twins kiss each other, this is not
a true kiss. The same holds true of a kiss given during Christ-

mas games, *item* of a stolen kiss. A kiss is a symbolic action which means nothing when the feeling it should indicate is not present, and this feeling can be present only under certain conditions.

If one wishes to attempt to classify the kiss, then one must take into consideration several principles of classification. One may classify it according to the sound. Unfortunately the element of language is inadequate in this respect to convey my observations. I do not believe that all the languages of the world have an adequate supply of onomatopoeic words to indicate the different sounds I have learned to know at my uncle's house alone. Sometimes the kiss is smacking, sometimes hissing, sometimes crackling, sometimes popping, sometimes booming, sometimes sonorous, sometimes hollow, sometimes like calico, and so on, and so on. One may also classify the kiss according to the contact, for example, the merely contiguous kiss or the kiss given *en passant,* and the cohesive kiss. One may classify the kiss according to the time element as the short and the long one. With reference to time there is still another classification possible, and this is really the only one I care about. One makes a distinction between the first kiss and all others. That which is meant here is incommensurable with whatever appears in connection with the other classifications; it is indifferent to sound, touch, time in general. The first kiss is, however, qualitatively different from all others. There are only a few people who think of this; it would therefore be a pity if there were not at least one person who makes reflections about it.

————————

My Cordelia!

A right answer is like a sweet kiss, says Solomon. You know I am much given to asking questions, I am almost taken to task for that. This is so because people do not understand what I ask; for you, and you alone, understand what I ask, and you, and you alone, understand how to answer, and you, and you alone, understand how to give a right answer. For a right answer is like a sweet kiss, says Solomon.

Your Johannes

There is a difference between spiritual love and physical love. Hitherto I have chiefly sought to develop the spiritual in Cordelia. My physical presence must now be something different, not just the accompanying mood, it must be a temptation. I have been constantly preparing myself in these days by reading the well-known passage about love in *Phaedrus*. It electrifies my whole being and is an excellent prelude. Plato really understood about the erotic.

My Cordelia!

The Latinist says of an attentive pupil that he hangs on his master's lips. For love everything is image and the image in turn is reality. Am I not a diligent, an attentive pupil? But you do not utter a single word.

Your Johannes

If someone other than myself were guiding this development, he would probably be too shrewd to allow himself to be guided. If I were to consult an initiate among those engaged, he would probably exclaim in an outburst of erotic boldness: I vainly seek among these positions of love for the one in which the lovers converse about their love. My answer would be: I am glad that you seek in vain, for this position simply does not belong within the scope of the intrinsically erotic, not even if one includes the interesting. Love is far too substantial to be content with talk; the erotic situations are far too significant to be filled up with talk. They are silent, still, with definite outlines, and yet as eloquent as the music of Memnon's pillar. Eros gestures, he does not speak, or if he does so, his speech consists of mysterious hinting, of a symbolic music. Erotic situations are always either plastic or graphic, but for two people to talk to each other about their love is neither plastic nor graphic. The conventionally engaged, however, always begin with such small talk, which eventually becomes the cement holding together their garrulous marriage. This small talk also provides assurance that their marriage will not lack the dowry Ovid mentions: *dos est uxoria lites* [nagging is the wife's dowry].

If there must be talking, it is sufficient for one partner to do it. The man ought to do the talking, and therefore he ought to be in possession of some of the powers inherent in the girdle with which Venus worked her charms: conversation and sweet insinuating flattery.

It follows by no means that Eros is mute or that it would be erotically incorrect to converse, but the conversation itself should be erotic, it should not lose itself in edifying speculations about the future, and the like, and it should be regarded essentially as a respite from the erotic act, a pastime, not as the main thing. Such a conversation, such a *confabulatio*, is truly divine in its nature, and I never get tired of talking with a young girl. What I mean is that I can get tired of this or that young girl, but never of talking with a young girl. That is just as impossible for me as to grow tired of breathing. The special quality of such a conversation is really its vegetative flowering. The conversation remains close to the ground, it is about nothing in particular, and the accidental is the law for its movements—it is like the daisy, common, but very charming.

My Cordelia!

"My—Your"—these words enclose the meager content of my letters like a parenthesis. Have you noticed that the space between its arms is growing shorter? Oh, my Cordelia! It is beautiful indeed that the emptier the parenthesis becomes, the more significant it becomes.

Your Johannes

My Cordelia!

Is an embrace combat?

Your Johannes

Generally Cordelia keeps silent. I have always liked that. She has too deep a feminine nature to plague one with hiatus, a figure of speech which is particularly characteristic of woman and which is inevitable when the man who should supply the preceding or succeeding limiting consonant is equally feminine. At times, however, a single brief utterance reveals how much is hidden in her soul, and then I render her help. It is as if behind a person making a rough sketch with unsteady hand there stood another who guided him and turned his hesitant strokes into something bold and finished. She is surprised, and yet it is as if the result belonged to her. Therefore I watch over her, over every casual utterance, every chance word, and when I give it back to her, it has always become

something more significant, something she both knows and
does not know.

Today we were together with others. We had not exchanged
a word with each other. We rose from the table; at this moment the servant came in and informed Cordelia that a messenger wished to speak with her. This messenger came from
me, he brought a letter which contained references to something I had said during the meal. I had managed to introduce
my remark into the general table conversation in such a way
that Cordelia, although she sat far away from me, could not
help overhearing it and misunderstanding it. The letter had
been planned with this contingency in mind. If I had not been
able to give the table conversation this turn, I should have
been present at the right moment to confiscate the letter. Upon
returning to the room, she had to tell a little lie. Such devices
consolidate the erotic secretiveness, without which she cannot
pursue the way assigned to her.

My Cordelia!

Do you believe that he who rests his head on Elverhøi, on
the Elfin Hill, sees the image of the elfin maiden in his dreams?
I do not know, but this I do know: when I rest my head upon
your bosom and gaze upward, I behold an angel's face. Do
you believe that he who rests his head on Elverhøi cannot lie
quiet? I do not believe it, but I do know that when I rest my
head upon your bosom, I am moved too deeply for sleep to
sink down upon my eyes.

Your Johannes

Jacta est alea [the die is cast]. Now the change must be
made. I was with her today, taken up with an idea that com-

pletely occupied my mind. I had neither eyes nor ears for her.
The idea was interesting in itself and fascinated her. Besides,
it would have been unwise to begin the new operation by being cold in her presence. When I have gone and the idea no
longer occupies her, she will easily realize that I was different
from my usual self. That she realizes the change when she is
by herself makes this discovery all the more painful; it will act
more slowly, but also more insidiously, upon her. She cannot
flare up immediately, and when the opportunity does come,
she will have thought of so much that she cannot express it all
at once, but will always retain a residuum of doubt. Her unrest increases, the letters cease, the erotic nourishment is diminished, and love is derided as an absurdity. Perhaps she goes
along with this for a short while, but in the long run she cannot endure it. She then strives to enchain me by the same
means I have used with her, by means of the erotic.

As regards the breaking off of an engagement, every little
girl is a perfect casuist, and although the schools offer no
courses in this subject, all girls are amazingly well informed
when the question is raised as to when an engagement ought
to be called off. This question ought to be asked regularly in
the school examinations of the senior year, and while I know
that the essays one usually gets in girls' schools are very monotonous, yet I am certain that here there would be no dearth of
variety, since the problem itself offers a wide scope for a girl's
acumen. And why should one not give a young girl the opportunity to display her acumen in the most brilliant manner?
Will she not in this way be able to show that she is mature—
mature enough to become engaged?

I once had an experience which I found highly interesting. One day I called on a family I sometimes visited, but the
elders had gone out, and the two young daughters of the house
had brought together a group of girl friends for a forenoon
coffee party. There were eight in all, ranging in age from sixteen to twenty. Probably they had not expected any visitors,

no doubt the maid had even received orders to say that nobody was at home. I did enter, however, and noticed clearly enough that they were somewhat surprised. God only knows what eight young girls like that really discuss at such a solemn synodical conference. Married women, too, occasionally get together in similar meetings. They then take up matters of pastoral theology, particularly such important problems as: when it is proper to let a maid go alone to the market, whether it is better to have an account with the butcher or to pay cash; whether it is likely that cook has a sweetheart, and how best to put a stop to the amorous goings-on in the kitchen, which cause delay in the preparation of meals.

I was asked to sit down in the midst of this lovely group. It was very early in the spring. The sun sent a few scattered rays as messengers of the season's approach. Inside everything was still winterly, and for this reason the isolated rays were especially full of promise. The coffee on the table spread its rich aroma—and the young girls themselves, well, they were happy, healthy, blooming, and light-headed, too, for their fear was soon allayed, and besides, what was there to be afraid of? After all, they had the advantage of numbers. I succeeded in turning their attention and the conversation to the question of the conditions under which an engagement ought to be broken. While my eye diverted itself by darting from one blossom to another in this circlet of maidens, while it diverted itself by resting now on one, now on another beauty, my outer ear reveled in the polyphony of their lovely voices and my inner ear took pleasure in listening to and analyzing what they had to say. A single word often sufficed to give me deep insight into such a girl's heart and its history. How seductive are the ways of love and how fascinating it is to investigate how far the individual has traveled along them! I constantly urged them on; cleverness, wit, aesthetic objectivity contributed their share to make the relationship more relaxed, and yet everything remained within the bounds of strictest decorum. While we frol-

icked thus in the airy regions of badinage, there hovered in
the background the possibility of causing these good children
no end of embarrassment with a single word. This possibility
lay within my reach. The girls did not realize this, they hardly
suspected it. Through the light play of the conversation this
possibility was constantly kept at a distance, just as Schehere-
zade staved off the execution of the death sentence with her
storytelling.

Sometimes I carried the conversation to the verge of melancholy; sometimes I let flippancy romp freely; sometimes I lured
them into a dialectical game. And what other subject possesses
so much multiplicity, offering something different from whatever angle one looks at it? I constantly suggested new themes.
I told about a girl who was forced by the cruelty of her parents to break her engagement. The unhappy conflict almost
brought tears to the eyes of my listeners. I told them about a
man who had given two reasons for having broken his engagement: the girl was too tall and he had not been down on his
knees while proposing. When I objected to him that these reasons could hardly be regarded as sufficient, he replied, "Yes,
they are just sufficient to accomplish what I want, for no one
can raise any reasonable objections to them."

I also presented a very difficult case for the consideration of
the company. A young girl broke her engagement, because she
felt convinced that she and her intended were not suited to
each other. The lover tried to bring her to reason by assuring
her that he loved her greatly, but she answered, "Either we
are suited to each other and real sympathy is present, and then
you will realize that we are not suited to each other, or we are
not suited to each other, and then you will realize that we are
not suited to each other."

It was a pleasure to observe how the young girls racked their
brains over this puzzling story, but I could also notice that a
couple of them understood it very well; for with regard to the
question of whether to break an engagement or not, every girl

is a born casuist. Yes, I truly believe that it would be easier for me to dispute with the devil himself than with a young girl when the subject is under what circumstances one ought to break an engagement.

Today I was with Cordelia. Hurriedly, with the speed of thought, I at once turned the conversation back to the same subject I had discussed with her yesterday, again trying to arouse ecstasy in her. "There was something I really wanted to say yesterday, but it did not occur to me until after I had gone." My device was successful. As long as I am with her, she enjoys listening to me; when I have left, she realizes that she has been cheated, that I am changed. Thus one gradually withdraws. This method is underhanded, but it serves the purpose excellently, like all indirect methods. She can easily explain to herself that I really find subjects like this one engrossing and that for the moment they also interest her, and yet I cheat her of the truly erotic.

Oderint, dum metuant [Let them hate, if only they fear]. As if only fear and hate belong together, while fear and love have nothing to do with each other! As if it were not fear that renders love interesting! With what kind of love do we embrace nature? Is there not a mysterious fear and terror in it, because its beautiful harmony rises from lawlessness and wild confusion, its security from perfidy? But this very fear is what is most fascinating. It is the same way with love if it is to be interesting. Beyond it there must brood the deep fearful night, from which the flower of love springs forth. Thus the *nymphaea alba* rests its chalice on the surface of the water, and thought dreads to plunge down into the deep darkness below, where it has its root.

I have noticed that she always addresses me with "my" when she writes to me, but she does not have the courage to say it to me. Today I begged her to do so, with all the insinuating and erotic warmth possible. She made a beginning, but an ironic glance, swifter and briefer than words can convey, was enough to make it impossible for her to continue, although my lips gave her every encouragement. This mood is normal.

She is mine. I do not confide this to the stars, as tradition prescribes. I do not really see how this information can be of concern to those distant spheres. Neither do I confide it to any human being, not even to Cordelia. This secret I keep to myself alone, I whisper it to myself in the very secret conversations I carry on with myself. The resistance attempted on her part was not particularly great; on the other hand, the erotic power she is developing is admirable. How interesting she is in this deep passionateness, how great she is, almost supernatural! How supple she is in evading, how lithe in insinuating herself wherever she discovers a defenseless point. Everything is in movement, but in this tumult of the elements I find myself precisely in my element. And yet she is by no means unbeautiful even in this upheaval, not dissipated in moods, not dispersed in moments. She is always an Anadyomene, except that she does not spring from the sea in naive charm or in serene calm, but agitated by the strong pulsations of love, while yet retaining unity and poise. Erotically she is fully equipped for the combat, she fights with the arrows of her eyes, with the command of her brows, with the mysteriousness of her forehead, with the eloquence of her bosom, with the dangerous allurement of her embrace, with the prayer on her lips, with the smile on her cheeks, with the sweet longing of her entire being. There is a power in her, an energy, as if she were a valkyrie, but this erotic vitality is in turn tempered by a certain languor which suffuses her.

Too long she must not be kept on this peak, where only anxiety and unrest can hold her upright and prevent her from collapsing. With such emotions she will soon feel that the engagement is too confining, too hampering. She herself becomes the tempter who seduces me to go beyond the bounds of the usual.

She becomes conscious of this, and for me that is the main thing.

Now she for her part drops numerous remarks which indicate that she is wearying of the engagement. They do not pass my ear unheeded; they are the scouts of my operation in her soul, who bring me enlightening hints; they are the ends of the threads by means of which I spin her into my plan.

My Cordelia!

You complain about the engagement. You think that our love does not need an external bond which serves only to hinder. Therein I immediately recognize my splendid Cordelia! I truly admire you. Our external union, after all, is only a separation. There is still a wall between us separating us like Pyramus and Thisbe. That people are privy to our secret is upsetting. Only in opposition is there freedom. When no outsider suspects that love exists, only then does it acquire significance. When every intruder believes that the lovers hate each other, only then is love happy.

Your Johannes

Soon the bond of the engagement will be severed. She herself will loosen it, in order, if possible, to bind me still more strongly with this looseness, just as flowing locks bind more securely than those piled high. If I were the one to break the engagement, I should deprive myself of this erotic *salto mortale*, which is so seductive to behold and so certain a sign of the boldness of her spirit. For me this is the main thing. An additional factor is that the whole incident would cause me all sorts of unpleasant consequences with respect to other people. I should become unpopular, people would hate and detest me, albeit unjustly, for such conduct on my part would prove advantageous to many. There is many a little spinster who, never having been engaged, would be content if she at least had been fairly close to an engagement. That, after all, is something, even though, to tell the truth, it is heartily little, for by the time one has elbowed oneself forward to get a place on the waiting list, there is little to wait for. The closer one moves to the top, the less one has to expect. In the world of love the principle of seniority does not hold. Such a little spinster, moreover, is tired of being in undivided possession of her estate, she urgently wants her life to be stirred by an event. But what can equal an unhappy love affair, particularly when one is not directly involved and therefore can take the matter lightly? Consequently she deludes herself and her neighbor into believing that she has been foully used, and since she is not eligible for admission to a Magdalen hospital, she treats herself to a crying jag. I am hated as a matter of duty.

To the above there must be added a division of those who have been wholly or half or three-quarters deceived. Many degrees are represented here, ranging from the girls who can point to a ring to those whose claims are based on the pressure of a hand during a contredanse. Their old wounds are torn open again by this new pain. I accept their hate along with the rest. But of course all these haters are so many crypto-lovers of my poor heart. A king without a country is a ridiculous figure, but a war of succession between a number of pretenders to a kingdom without a country, that surpasses even what is most ridiculous. Hence I ought really to be loved and patronized by the fair sex as if I were a pawnshop. A man actually engaged can take care of only one girl, but such an unlimited possibility can provide for, that is to say, can tolerably well provide for, any number at will. All this limited nonsense I now get rid of, and at the same time I have the advantage of being able afterwards to appear in an entirely new role. The young girls will pity me, sympathize with me, sigh for me, and I shall make music with them in the same key. Also in this way can one make conquests.

Strange indeed! I notice now to my chagrin that I am getting the revealing sign which Horace wished on all faithless girls—a black tooth, and a front tooth at that. How superstitious can one be! The tooth really upsets me, I cannot stand any reference to it; this touchiness is a weak side I have. While in all other respects I am fully armed, here even the greatest lout can cause me far deeper suffering than he imagines when he touches on this tooth. I do everything possible to make it white, but all in vain. I say with Palnatoke:

> I rub it by night and by day,
> But I cannot rub this black shadow away.

Life certainly holds an extraordinary amount of mystery. Such a little circumstance can upset me more than the most dangerous attack, the most embarrassing situation. I'll have it extracted, although this is going to have a bad effect on my voice and its power. Well, I shall have it replaced with a false one. It will be false to the world; the black one was false to me.

It is an excellent thing that Cordelia is taking offense at the state of being engaged. Marriage will always be a venerable institution, although it possesses the tedium of already enjoying in its youth part of the venerability acquired by old age. An engagement, however, is a purely human invention, and as such it is so prodigious and ridiculous that on the one hand it is entirely in order that a young girl should ignore it in the whirl of passion, and yet on the other hand sense its significance, feel her soul's energy present everywhere in herself as a higher circulatory system. What is important now is to guide her in such a way that in her bold flight she loses sight of marriage and the mainland of reality in general, that her soul, just as much in its pride as in its fear of losing me, destroys an imperfect human convention in order to hasten to something higher than the common level of humanity. In this respect, however, I have nothing to fear, for she already traverses life in such an ethereal and light manner that reality to a great extent is lost sight of. Besides, I am constantly on board and can always stretch the sails.

Woman is and will always be for me an inexhaustible source for reflection, an eternal store for observation. The man who does not feel the urge to conduct this study, whatever he may be in the world, one thing he certainly is not: an aesthetician. This is precisely the glory and divinity of aesthetics, that it enters into relation with the beautiful only, that by its very nature it is concerned with belles-lettres and the fair sex only. It makes me glad, it makes my heart glad, when I represent to myself the sun of womanhood irradiating in infinite manifoldness, spreading a Babel-like confusion, where each individual woman possesses a small portion of womanhood's vast wealth, yet in such a way that all her other qualities center harmoniously about this part. In this sense feminine beauty is infinitely divisible. But the individual portion of beauty must be harmoniously controlled, otherwise the effect is disturbing, and one gains the impression that nature had intended something or other with the girl in question, but nothing came of the intention.

My eyes can never weary of hastening over this peripheral manifoldness, these scattered emanations of feminine beauty. Each separate part has its little share, and yet is perfect in itself, happy, blithe, beautiful. Every woman has her portion: the merry smile, the roguish glance, the yearning eye, the drooping head, the exuberant temperament, the quiet melancholy, the deep foreboding, the brooding hypochondria, the earthly nostalgia, the unconfessed stirrings, the beckoning brows, the questioning lips, the mysterious forehead, the captivating curls, the concealing lashes, the heavenly pride, the earthly modesty, the angelic purity, the secret blush, the light step, the graceful glide, the languishing posture, the longing revery, the unexplained sighs, the willowy shape, the soft forms, the voluptuous bosom, the swelling hips, the small foot, the dainty hand. Each woman has her share, and what the one does not have the other has.

When I have seen and seen again, considered and considered again, this feminine world's manifoldness, when I have smiled, sighed, cajoled, threatened, desired, tempted, laughed, wept, hoped, feared, won, and lost—then I fold up the fan, then the scattered elements are gathered into a unity, the parts into a whole. Then my soul rejoices, then my heart throbs, then passion is aflame. This one girl, the only one in the whole world, she must belong to me, she must be mine. Let God keep His heaven, if only I may keep her. Well I know what I choose; it is something so great that heaven would suffer irreparably from such a separation, for what would be left to heaven if I kept her? The faithful Mohammedans would be disappointed in their hopes when in their paradise they embraced pale, weak shadows. Warm hearts they would not be able to find, for all the warmth of the heart would be gathered in her breast; disconsolate, they would despair when they found pale lips, lusterless eyes, an inert bosom, a limp pressure of the hand, for all the redness of the lips and the fire of the eyes and the unrest of the bosom and the promise conveyed by the pressure of the hand and the premonition of the sigh and the seal of the kiss and the trembling contact and the passion of the embrace—all, all would be concentrated in her, who would lavish on me a wealth sufficient for this world and the next.

Thus I have often thought about the matter, but every time I do so, I grow fervid, because I think of her as fervid. But although in general ardency is accounted a good sign, it does not follow from this that my mode of thinking will be granted the honorable predicate of sound. Therefore I, who now for variety's sake am cold, shall think of her as cold. I shall try to think of woman categorically. Under what category must she be conceived? Under that of being for another. This, however, must not be understood in a bad sense, as if the woman who is for me would also be for another. Here as always in abstract thinking, one must refrain from every reference to experience, for otherwise I should have experience both for me and against me in a strange manner.

Here as everywhere experience is something strange, for its nature is always to be both for and against. Woman, then, is being for another. But here again one must not let oneself be confused from another side by experience, which teaches that one rarely encounters a woman who is truly being for another, since as a rule a great many are nothing at all, either for themselves or for others. This design woman has in common with all of nature and with everything feminine in general. Nature as a whole exists only for another, not in the teleological sense that one specific part of nature exists for another specific part, but in the sense that nature as whole exists for another—for the spirit. The same holds true for the separate parts. Plant life, for example, unfolds its hidden charms in all naïveté and exists only for another. In the same way, a puzzle, a charade, a secret, a vowel, and so on, have being solely for another. From this it can be explained why God, when He created Eve, caused a deep sleep to fall upon Adam, for woman is man's dream. In still another way we can learn from this story that woman is being for another. It tells, namely, that Jehovah took one of Adam's ribs. Had she, for example, been taken from man's brain, woman would indeed have continued to be being for another, but the intention was not that she should be a figment of the brain, but something totally different. She became flesh and blood, but this causes her to come under the category of nature, which is essentially being for another. She first awakens at the touch of love; before this time she is a dream. Two stages, however, can be distinguished in this dream existence: in the first stage love dreams about her, in the second, she dreams about love.

As being for another, woman is characterized by pure virginity. Virginity is a being which, insofar as it is being for itself, is really an abstraction and only reveals itself to another. The same also holds true of female innocence. One can therefore say that woman in this condition is invisible. As is well known, there existed no image of Vesta, the goddess who most nearly represented the essence of virginity. This existence is jealous for itself aesthetically, just as Jehovah is jealous ethically, and does not desire that there should be any image or even any idea of itself. This is the contradiction, that what is for another, is not, and only becomes visible, as it were, through that another. Logically, this contradiction is quite in order, and he who knows how to think logically will not be upset by it, but will take delight in it. Whoever thinks illogically, on the other hand, will imagine that whatever is being for another *is*, in the finite sense in which one can say about a particular thing: it is something for me.

This being of woman (the word *existence* says too much, for woman does not exist of herself) is correctly characterized as charm, a term which suggests the vegetative life; she is like a flower, as the poets are wont to say, and even the spiritual in her is present in a vegetative manner. She is wholly determined by nature and therefore only aesthetically free. In a deeper sense she first becomes free through man, and therefore one says: *at frie* and therefore the man *frier*.* When he woos properly, there can be no question of any choice. Woman chooses, it is true, but if this choosing is thought of as the result of a long deliberation, then such choosing is unfeminine. Therefore it is disgraceful to be rejected, because the individual involved has rated himself too high, has desired to make another free

---

* A play on *fri* (free) and *at fri(e)* (to woo).

without being able to do so.—In this situation there lies a deep irony. That which is for another acquires the appearance of being the predominant element: man woos, woman chooses. It is inherent in the concept of woman that she be the vanquished, it is inherent in the concept of man that he be the victor, and yet the victor bows before the vanquished, and yet this is quite natural, and only churlishness, stupidity, and lack of erotic sensibility can disregard what follows spontaneously in this fashion. There is also a deeper reason: woman is substance, man is reflection. She therefore does not choose directly, but the man woos, she chooses. But man's wooing is a questioning, and her choosing is really only an answer to a question. In a certain sense man is more than woman, in another sense infinitely less.

This being for another is pure virginity. If it makes an attempt to be itself in relation to another being that is being for it, then the difference reveals itself in absolute primness, but this difference shows at the same time that woman's essential being is being for another. The diametrical opposite to absolute devotion is absolute primness, which, in a converse sense, is invisible as the abstraction against which everything shatters, without the abstraction for that reason coming to life. Femininity now acquires the character of abstract cruelty, which is the extreme form taken by virginal prudery. A man can never be so cruel as a woman. Consult mythologies, fairy tales, folk legends, and you will find this confirmed. If the aim is to describe a natural force whose mercilessness knows no bounds, this force always assumes the form of a virginal being. Or one is horrified to read of a maiden who callously allows her suitors to lose their lives, as so often happens in the fairy tales of all peoples. A Bluebeard kills each of the women he has enjoyed on her wedding night, but he does not enjoy killing her; on the contrary, his joy has preceded the killing. Therein lies the concretion, it is not cruelty for cruelty's sake.

A Don Juan seduces them and leaves them, but he finds no joy in leaving them, his joy lies in seducing them; his cruelty therefore is by no means this abstract cruelty.

The more I reflect on this matter, the more I am convinced that my practice is in perfect harmony with my theory. My practice has always been impregnated with the conviction that woman is essentially being for another. Therefore the moment has here such infinite significance, for being for another is always the matter of a moment. It may take a longer or shorter time before the moment comes, but as soon as it has come, that which originally was being for another becomes a relative being, and that is the end. Well I know that husbands say that the woman also is being for another in another sense, that she is everything for them through life. One must make allowances for husbands. I am inclined to think that this is something they make one another believe. Every social class has certain conventional customs and particularly certain conventional lies. Among the latter must be reckoned this tall tale. To be a judge of the moment is no easy matter, and he who misjudges it must, of course, put up with a boring companion for the rest of his life. The moment is everything, and in the moment woman is everything; the consequences I do not understand. Among these is the consequence of getting children. Now I like to imagine that I am a fairly consequential thinker, but even if I were to become mad, I am not the man to think this consequence; I simply do not understand it. For this a husband is necessary.

Yesterday Cordelia and I visited a family at their summer residence. The party spent most of the time in the garden, where it entertained itself with all sorts of games requiring physical skill. Among other things, we played ring-throwing. When a man, who had been playing with Cordelia, left, I took his place. What a wealth of charm she revealed, even more seductive because the game's exertion enhanced her beauty! What graceful harmony in the self-contradiction of her move-

ments! How light they were—like a dance over meadows! How
vigorous, yet without requiring resistance, how deceptive until
her restored poise explained everything! How dithyrambic was
her appearance, how challenging her glance!

The game itself naturally had a special interest for me. Cordelia did not seem to pay much attention to it. An allusion I
made to one of the persons present to the beautiful custom of
exchanging the rings struck her soul like a bolt of lightning.
From this moment a higher radiance was spread over the entire situation, a deeper significance impregnated it, an intenser
energy inspired her. I held both rings on my stick, I paused
for a moment and exchanged a few words with the bystanders.
She understood this pause. I again tossed the rings to her, and
she caught both of them on her stick. Then, as if inadvertently,
she cast the two rings straight up into the air at the same
time, so high that it was impossible for me to catch them. This
throw was accompanied by a glance full of infinite audacity.
They tell a story about a French soldier who had taken part in
the campaign in Russia and whose leg had to be amputated
because of gangrene. As soon as the painful operation was
over, he seized the leg by the sole of the foot, cast it up into the
air, and shouted: *Vive l'empereur!* With a similar look she,
more beautiful than ever before, cast both rings into the air
and said to herself: Long live love! I, however, found it inad-
visable to let her be carried away by this mood or to leave her
alone in it, for fear of the weariness that so often follows it. I
therefore remained quite calm and, aided by the presence of
the bystanders, obliged her to continue playing, as if I had
noticed nothing. Such conduct gives her even more elasticity.

If in our age one could expect a certain amount of interest in
investigations of this type, I should pose the prize question: aesthetically considered, who is the more modest, a young girl or a
young matron, the unknowing or the knowing, and to whom
may one grant more freedom? But such matters do not occupy
the attention of our serious age. In ancient Greece such an in-

quiry would have aroused general attention, the whole state
would have been agog, particularly the young girls and the
young matrons. In our skeptical age it would be difficult to
induce people to believe that in antiquity there once took place
a well-known contest between two Greek girls and that this
occasioned an extremely thorough investigation, for in Greece
one did not treat such problems lightly and carelessly. Yet
everybody knows that Venus has a sobriquet as a result of this
contest, and everybody admires the statue of Venus bearing
and immortalizing this name.

A married woman has two periods in her life when she is interesting: her earliest youth and much later, when she has
grown considerably older. But she also has—one must not deny
her this—a moment when she is even more charming and inspires even more respect than a young girl, but this is a moment which rarely occurs in life, it is a picture for the inner
eye which does not need to be seen in life and which perhaps
never is seen. I visualize her as healthy, blooming, voluptuous;
she holds a child on her arm, toward whom her whole attention is directed, in whose contemplation she is lost. It is a picture which one may describe as the loveliest that human life
has to offer, it is a myth of nature, which must therefore be
seen in a representation, not in reality. There must, furthermore, be no additional figures in the picture, no setting, which
would merely serve to distract. If one betakes oneself into our
churches, one frequently has occasion to witness a baptism,
where the mother steps forward with the child on her arm.
Even if he managed to disregard the disconcerting wail of the
infant and to repress the unpleasant thoughts aroused by the
expectations of the parents for the future of the little one,
based on the volume of its cry, he would still find the surroundings so confusing that the effect would be lost. He sees
the father, which is a great drawback, as it cancels the mythi-
cal element, the enchantment; he sees—*horrenda refero*—the
sponsors' solemn chorus, and he sees—nothing at all. On the

other hand, there is nothing more charming than the image of mother and child presented to the imagination as a picture. I lack neither the boldness nor the rashness necessary to venture an attack—but if I saw such a picture in reality, I would be completely disarmed.

How Cordelia engrosses me! And yet the time is soon over; my soul requires constant rejuvenation. Already I seem to hear the distant crowing of the cock. Perhaps she hears it too, but she believes that it heralds the morning.—Why is a young girl so pretty, and why does this state last such a short time? I could become quite melancholy over this thought, and yet, after all, it is no concern of mine. Enjoy, do not talk. The people who make a profession of such reflections generally do not enjoy. However, it can do no harm to harbor this thought, for the sadness it evokes, a sadness not for one's self but for others, generally makes one a little more handsome in a masculine way. A sadness which broods deceptively like a veil of mist over manly strength is an essential part of the masculine erotic. In woman there is a corresponding melancholy.

When a girl has given herself entirely, then everything is over. I still approach a young girl with a certain anxiety, my heart throbs, because I feel the eternal power in her being. In the presence of a woman I have never felt like this. The slight resistance she tries to offer with the help of art amounts to nothing at all. It is as if one were to say that the cap of a married woman was more impressive than the uncovered head of a young girl. For that reason Diana has always been my ideal. This pure virginity, this absolute primness has always fascinated me. But while she has always held my attention, I have at the same time harbored a secret grudge against her. I cannot help believing that she has not really deserved all the encomia bestowed upon her because of her virginity. She knew, namely, that her role in life depended upon her preserving her virginity. I must also mention that in a remote philological corner of the world I heard a rumor to the effect that she knew about the terrible birth pains her mother had suffered and that this frightened her greatly. I cannot hold this against Diana, I merely say with Euripides: I would rather go to war three times than bear one child. To be sure, I could not fall in love with Diana, but I do not deny that I would give much for a conversation with her, for what one might call an aboveboard conversation. No doubt she would be good for all sorts of teasing tricks. My good Diana obviously possesses a knowledge that makes her far less naive even than Venus. I should not care to spy on her while she is bathing, not at all, but I should like to spy on her with my questions. If I were stealing off to a rendezvous with her where I feared for my victory, I should prepare myself and arm myself, and I should set all the spirits of love in motion by conversing with her.

A frequent subject of reflection on my part has been what situation, what moment may be regarded as the most seductive one. The answer to this naturally depends upon what one desires and how one desires and what one's development has been. My choice is the wedding day, and especially a particular moment on that day. When she stands there in her bridal adornment and all this splendor pales before her own beauty, and she herself turns pale, when the blood stops to flow, when the bosom rests, when the glance falters, when the foot is unsteady, when the maiden trembles, when the fruit ripens; when heaven exalts her, when earnestness fortifies her, when the promise supports her, when prayer blesses her, when the myrtle crowns her; when the heart throbs, when the eyes look down at the ground, when she hides herself within herself, when she does not belong to the world in order to belong to it completely; when the bosom heaves, when the whole figure sighs, when the voice fails, when the tear quivers, before the enigma is explained, when the torch is lighted, when the bridegroom waits—then the moment has arrived. Soon it will be too late. Only one step remains to be taken, but this is exactly enough for a false step. This moment makes even an insignificant girl significant, even a little Zerlina becomes an object. Everything must be gathered together, the most disparate elements must be united in the moment; if there is something lacking, particularly one of the chief opposites, then the situation immediately loses a part of its seductiveness.

There is a well-known engraving representing a penitent. She looks so young and so innocent that one wonders what she can have to confess and nearly feels embarrassment on her account and her confessor's. She raises her veil a little and looks out into the world as if she were looking for something she might be able to confess on some future occasion, and it really goes without saying that to do so is no more than her duty out of consideration for—the father confessor. The situation is quite seductive, and since she is the only figure in the piece, there is nothing to prevent one's imagining the church in which all this is taking place to be so spacious that a good many greatly different preachers could easily preach there at the same time. The situation is quite seductive, and I have no objection to placing myself in the background, especially if the girl has no objection. However, it remains a highly subordinate position, for the girl does seem to be only a child in both directions, and consequently a great deal of time will have to pass before the moment arrives.

Have I in my relation to Cordelia always been faithful to my pact? That is to say: my pact with the aesthetic, for what makes me strong is that I always have the idea on my side. This is a secret like Samson's hair, a secret no Delilah shall wrest from me. I would certainly lack the perseverance necessary actually to betray a girl, but that the idea is involved, that it is in its service I act, that it is to its service I dedicate myself, all this enables me to be severe toward myself, to abstain from every forbidden enjoyment. Has the interesting always been preserved? Yes, in this secret conversation with myself I may say freely and openly that it has been. The engagement itself was interesting precisely because it did not offer that which one generally understands by the interesting. It preserved the interesting precisely because the outward appearance was in contradiction to the inward life. Had I been secretly bound to her, it would have been interesting in the first power only. This, however, is the interesting in the second power, and only for this reason does it become the interesting for her. The engagement is broken, but this is because she herself breaks it in order to elevate herself to a higher sphere. Thus shall it be, for this is the form of the interesting which will occupy her most.

The bond has burst. Full of yearning, strong, bold, divine, she flies like a bird which now for the first time may spread its wings their full breadth. Fly, bird, fly! Verily, if this royal flight were a withdrawal from me, it would cause me profound pain. It would be for me as if Pygmalion's beloved were again turned to stone. Light have I made her, light as a thought, and now this, my own thought should no longer belong to me! That would plunge me into despair. A moment sooner it would not have mattered to me, a moment later it shall not worry me, but now—now—this now, which is an eternity for me! Fly, then, bird, fly, soar proudly on your wings, glide along through the soft realms of the air! Soon I shall be with you, soon I shall conceal myself with you in deep solitude!

The aunt was somewhat taken aback by the news. She is too liberal, however, to try to force Cordelia, although I, partly to lull her into an even deeper sleep, partly to tease Cordelia a little, have made an attempt to get her to become interested in me. For the rest, she shows me much sympathy; she does not suspect how much reason I have for declining all sympathy.

Cordelia has obtained permission from her aunt to spend some time in the country, where she will visit a family. It is fortunate that she cannot immediately abandon herself to the rapture of her mood. For some time she will continue to be kept in a state of tension by all kinds of resistance from outside. I maintain desultory contact with her by means of letters;

in this way our relationship is kept alive. She must now be made strong in every way; it will be best to allow her to indulge in a few gestures expressing her contempt of people and of the ordinary. Then when the day for her departure arrives, a reliable fellow will turn up to serve as coachman. Outside the gate my absolutely trustworthy servant will join them. He will accompany her to the place of destination and will remain with her to wait on her and assist her whenever necessary. Next to myself I know no one who is better suited for this than Johan. I myself have arranged everything out there as tastefully as possible. Nothing is lacking which can in any way serve to fascinate her soul and soothe it with a sense of luxuriant well-being.

My Cordelia!

Not yet have the cries of "Fire!" from individual families merged into the confusion of a deafening Capotiline cackle of alarm. No doubt you have already had to endure a few solo outbursts. Just imagine the whole assembly of tea addicts and coffee fiends, imagine the lady who presides and who is a worthy counterpart to that immortal President Lars in the works of Claudius, and you have a picture and an idea of what you have lost and with whom you have lost it: the esteem of good people.

With this letter I enclose the famous engraving which represents President Lars. I was unable to purchase it separately, and so I bought the Claudius volume, tore it out, and threw the rest away, for how would I dare to trouble you with a gift which has no significance for you at this time? How would I not do my utmost to procure for you something which may give you pleasure, if only for a moment? How would I permit more to enter into the situation than belongs to it?

Nature has such an amorphousness, and so has the man who is bound by all the finite conditions of life; but you, my Cordelia, will hate it in your freedom.

                                                    Your Johannes

———————

Spring is the most beautiful season of the year in which to fall in love; autumn the most beautiful in which to reach the goal of one's desires. In the autumn season there is a melancholy that corresponds entirely to the emotion with which the thought of the fulfillment of our desires suffuses us. To-day I was out at the country place where in a few days Cordelia will find an environment in harmony with her soul. I myself do not desire to share her surprise and pleasure over this; such erotic distractions would only weaken her soul. On the other hand, when she is alone with them, she will pass her time in revery, everywhere she will see allusions, intimations, an enchanted world. But all this would lose its significance if I stood beside her, it would cause her to forget that for us the period of time when such things enjoyed in fellowship had significance lies behind us. This new environment must not narcotize her soul, rather must it constantly let her soul rise up and look down upon it as upon a game which has no significance in comparison with what is to come. I, for my part, intend in these remaining days to visit this place frequently in order to keep myself in the mood.

———————

My Cordelia!

Now I truly call you *mine*. No external sign reminds me of my possession.—Soon I call you truly *mine*. And when I hold you tightly enclosed in my arms, when you entwine me in your embrace, then we need no ring to remind us that we belong to each other, for is not this embrace a ring which is more than a mere sign? And the more tightly this ring encloses us, the more inseparably it joins us together, the greater the freedom, for your freedom consists in being mine, just as my freedom consists in being yours.

Your Johannes

My Cordelia!

While hunting, Alpheus fell in love with the nymph Arethusa. She would not grant his prayer, but constantly fled before him, until on the island of Ortygia she was changed into a spring. Alpheus' grief over this was so great that he was changed into a river in Elis in the Peloponnesus. He did not forget his love, however, but mingled with that spring under the sea. Is the time of metamorphoses past? Answer: Is the time of love past? With what should I compare your pure deep soul, which has no connection with the world, if not with a spring? And have I not said to you that I am like a river which has fallen in love? And now that we are separated, do I not plunge under the sea to be united with you? Under the sea, there we meet again, for only in this depth do we really belong together.

Your Johannes

My Cordelia!

Soon, soon you will be mine. When the sun shuts its spying eye, when history is over and the myths begin, then not only do I fling my cloak about me, I also fling the night about me like a cloak, and hasten to you, and listen, in order to find you, not for the sound of footsteps, but for the pounding of the heart.

Your Johannes

In these days when I cannot be together with her in person whenever I wish, the thought has disturbed me that it might occur to her to think of the future. So far it has never occurred to her to do so, for I have known too well how to drug her aesthetically. Nothing less erotic can be imagined than this talk about the future, the reason for which usually is that one has nothing wherewith to fill the present. Once I am on the scene, I do not fear such an eventuality, for I am well able to make her forget both time and eternity. If a man does not understand how to put himself in rapport with a girl to that extent, then he should never try to cast a spell over her, then it will be impossible to avoid the two perilous rocks: questions about the future and catechization about matters of faith. It therefore was quite as it should be for Gretchen to subject Faust to such an examination, since he had been imprudent enough to play the cavalier, and against such an attack a girl is always armed.

Now I believe everything is ready for her reception. She shall not lack occasion to admire my memory, or rather she shall not have the time to admire it. Nothing is forgotten which could have any significance for her, and on the other hand, nothing is introduced which might remind her of me directly, although I am invisibly present everywhere. The effect, however, will largely depend on the impression she gains when she sees everything for the first time. In this connection my servant has received the most exact instructions, and he is in his way an accomplished virtuoso. He knows how to drop a remark casually and carelessly when he has been told to do so; he knows how to be ignorant; in short, I find him invaluable.

The site could not be more to her liking. If one sits in the center of the room, one can look out beyond the foreground in both directions, on both sides one has the endless horizon, one is alone in the sky's wide sea. If one moves closer to the row of windows, then one sees the arch of a forest on the distant horizon, limiting and enclosing. This is just as it should be. What does Love love? An enclosed place. Was not Paradise itself an enclosed place, a garden facing the east? But the enclosing ring becomes too tight, becomes oppressive— one steps still closer to the window. A quiet lake lies humbly hidden within the higher surroundings; on the shore lies a boat. A sigh from the fullness of the heart, a gasp relieving the thought's unrest, and the boat loosens itself from its moorings, it glides over the lake's surface, gently carried along by the mild breeze of ineffable longing. One disappears into the mysterious solitude of the forest, rocked by the surface of the lake dreaming of the forest's deep darkness. Now one turns to the other side; there the lake spreads out before one's eyes, which nothing prevents from roaming freely, while the mind pursues thoughts which nothing restrains.—What does Love love? Infiniteness. What does Love fear? Limitation.

Beyond the large room there is a smaller one, really a cabinet, for this chamber is what the corresponding room in the Wahl residence was meant to be. The similarity is striking. A carpet woven of osiers covers the floor; before the sofa stands a small tea table with a lamp like the one she has at home. Everything is the same, only richer. Surely I may allow myself the luxury of this difference. In the salon stands a piano, a very plain one, but it is reminiscent of the piano in the Jansen household. The keyboard is open. On the music rest are the notes of the little Swedish air.

The door leading to the entry stands ajar. Johan has been

instructed to see to it that she enters through the door in the background. Her glance takes in the cabinet and the piano at the same time. Memory awakens in her soul. At this moment Johan opens wide the other door. The illusion is complete. She enters the cabinet. She is pleased with what she finds, I am sure of that. As she glances at the table, she sees a book. At this very moment Johan picks it up as if to put it away, saying casually, "The master must have forgotten it when he was out here this morning." In this way she gets to know that I was there before her in the course of the morning. She then looks at the book. It is a German translation of the well-known work by Apuleius, *Amor and Psyche*. It is not poetry, but the intention is not to offer her poetry at this time, for it is always an insult to a young girl to offer her an actual poetical work, as if in such a moment she were not sufficiently poetical to absorb the poetry which is inherent in the given situation and which has not yet been assimilated by another's thought. People as a rule do not consider this, and yet it is so.—She will read the book, which is why it has been put there. When she opens it at the place where it was last read, she will find a little sprig of myrtle; she will also find that it is meant to be a little more than just a bookmark.

My Cordelia!

Why feel fear? When we keep together, then we are strong, stronger than the world, stronger than the gods themselves. You know there once lived a race of creatures on earth, who were human beings, to be sure, but each one of whom was sufficient unto himself and did not know the inner union of love. Yet they were mighty, so mighty that they wanted to take heaven by storm. Jupiter feared them and divided them in such a way that from one came two, a man and a woman.

If now it sometimes happens that what was once united is again joined together in love, then such a union is stronger than Jupiter. The man and woman thus united are not only as strong as the pristine being was, they are even stronger, for love's union is an even higher one.

Your Johannes

Sept. 24th.

The night is still. It is a quarter of twelve. The watchman by the gate blows his benediction out over the open country; the sound echoes back from the Blegdam. He enters the gate, he blows again, the echo comes from farther away. Everything sleeps in peace, everything except love. Then arise, you mysterious powers of love, gather in this breast! The night is silent—a lonely bird interrupts this silence with its cry and the beat of its wings, as it skims over the dewy field down the incline of the glacis; no doubt it, too, is hastening to a trysting place. *Accipio omen!* How portentous all nature is! I take note of the omen in the flight of the birds, in their cries, in the lively flapping of the fishes against the surface of the water, in their vanishing down below, in the distant barking of dogs, in the faraway rumble of a carriage, in footsteps echoing from afar.

I do not see specters in this nocturnal hour, I do not see what has been but what will be, in the bosom of the lake, in the kiss of the dew, in the mist which spreads out over the earth and hides its fertile embrace. Everything is symbol; I myself am a myth about myself, for is it not as a myth that I hasten to this reunion? Who I am contributes nothing of importance; everything finite and temporal is forgotten, only the eternal remains, the power of love, its yearning, its ecstasy.

How my soul is tautened like a drawn bow, how my thoughts lie ready like arrows in a quiver, not poisoned, but well suited to blend with the blood! How vigorous is my soul, how sound,

joyous, present like a god!—Nature endowed Cordelia with
beauty. I thank you, wondrous Nature! Like a mother you
watched over her. Accept my gratitude for your loving care!
Unspoiled was she. I thank you, oh human beings, to whom
she is indebted for this. Her development was my work—soon
I shall enjoy my reward.—How much I have gathered into
this one moment which now draws near. Damnation, if it
should escape me!

I do not see my carriage.—I hear the crack of a whip, it is
my coachman.—Drive now for dear life, no matter if the
horses collapse, provided they do not do so before we reach
our destination.

Sept. 25th.

Why cannot such a night last longer? If Alectryon could forget himself, why cannot the sun be compassionate enough to do the same? Still, it is over now, and I do not want ever to see her again. When a girl has given away·everything, then she is weak, then she has lost everything. In the case of a man, innocence is a negative moment; in the case of a woman, it is the very content of her being. Now all resistance is impossible, and only as long as that is present, is it beautiful to love; when it has ceased, there remain only weakness and habit. I do not care to be reminded of my relation to her; she has lost her fragrance, and the times are gone when a girl was changed into a heliotrope because of sorrow over her faithless lover. I don't want to take leave of her, for there is nothing more revolting than the tears and lamentations of women, which change everything and yet really mean nothing. I have loved her, but from now on she can no longer occupy my soul. Were I a god, I would do for her what Neptune did for a nymph: change her into a man.

There is one thing, however, which it would be worthwhile to know: is it possible to abandon a girl in such a way that she would imagine proudly that it was she who was breaking off the relationship because she had grown tired of it all? This would provide a fascinating epilogue, which would be of great psychological interest and enable one to make many valuable observations of an erotic nature.